James Rush

Rhymes of contrast on wisdom and folly

James Rush

Rhymes of contrast on wisdom and folly

ISBN/EAN: 9783337270254

Printed in Europe, USA, Canada, Australia, Japan

Cover: Foto ©Andreas Hilbeck / pixelio.de

More available books at **www.hansebooks.com**

RHYMES OF CONTRAST

ON

WISDOM AND FOLLY.

A COMPARISON BETWEEN

OBSERVANT AND REFLECTIVE AGE,

DERISIVELY CALLED FOGIE,

AND A

SENSELESS AND UNTHINKING AMERICAN GO-AHEAD

INTENDED TO EXEMPLIFY

AN IMPORTANT AGENT IN THE WORKING PLAN

OF THE

HUMAN INTELLECT.

A NARRATED DIALOGUE.

BY JAMES RUSH, M.D.,

AUTHOR OF A 'NATURAL HISTORY OF THE INTELLECT,' THE 'PHILOSOPHY
OF THE HUMAN VOICE,' AND OF 'HAMLET,
A DRAMATIC PRELUDE.'

PHILADELPHIA:
J. B. LIPPINCOTT & CO.
FEBRUARY FIRST,
MDCCCLXIX.

PREFACE.

THROUGH ignorance or inattention, the purpose of an act may be at first and afterwards overlooked; as will probably be the case with the following Pages. I do not publish them with reference to their Anapestic canter and jingle, their humor, oddity, or even the needed satire they may contain: which whether passable or indifferent, are not offered as 'something new,' that eye and ear-trap of the day. Regarding the execution of such subjects, others have already treated them better than falls within the Author's ability. The most trifling fiction may however, illustrate the most important truth; and if the mere literary critic overlooking the intention of the trifle before him, should successfully retort jest and ridicule against its invasive attack upon folly, ignorance, and vice, it would require no great effort: for wit, whatever its originality or power, can always be answered by wit, rendered brighter perhaps by the light it was designed to extinguish. And here so different from the steadfastness of truth, which cannot be opposed, and only confirmed by truth; ridicule being no test of it, except made by the tongue of truth, and then it will be no humorous contrast to itself. Though truth may be acceptably caricatured by drollery, it is always from the painter and spectator seeing its misrepresentation under an ignorance of its real form and action: truth seeming then contorted and ridiculous, because it is so to the habit of their imperfect and limited perceptions.

I make these remarks previously to stating the purpose of the following rhymes; and if it is not regarded, we must consider the Reader one of those Precipitators, whether young or old, who run so fast, and look so exclusively after their own object, as to be unable to notice what is deliberate and practical.

Many pages in the 'Natural History of the Intellect,' particularly in the thirty-third section, describe what is there called the 'Natural or Related Tie' of perception: the meaning of which however, can be fully comprehended only by a perusal of that Work. If the Reader has not seen it, which is more than probable, for its truths have been outlawed by a set of metaphysical 'logicians' of feeble muscle, rickety bone, and most excitable skin, he must now be told it is there described as a necessary connection that one image on the brain has with another, though the cause and manner of the connection are unknown; this natural tie being a contributive function in every connected production of thought. It is in part, and obscurely described by the old metaphysicians, under the phrase 'Association of Ideas.' The natural tie however, in the above-named history, is systematically pointed out, and its method and effects are often particularly illustrated. It is there shown to be altogether an *involuntary* connection or other relation between one or more of the images of things

on the brain, under the like Laws of Nature that govern the
rest of the Universe; which are not at the command of human
power, but so to call them, are the ordination, or the direc-
tive choice of God and Nature.   I mean to say, that when
the thought of paper currency brings up the thought of folly,
extravagance, vice, and ruin; or the thought of a Legislator
brings up that of bribery; or the thought of America that of
a restless and perpetually changing, building up, tearing down,
and gadding people; these several connections are in our
view a necessary result of a law of the brain, and therefore
cannot be prevented by any influence of the Will.   Hence I
have described that connection as the natural, or involuntary,
or related tie between the images of thought.

These ties under the name of 'Association,' have by the
Schoolmen been arranged and named from connections of resemblance, cause and effect, contrast, contrariety, habit, words,
and other relations that bring together images on the human
brain.   But these divisions are less worthy of attention than
the fact of their being involuntary; which under the Laws of
Nature, connects the images of thoughts and words, in the
physical working plan of the brain, and rejects the supposed
free-will choice of a metaphysical Spirit.   This conscious
spirit has, to perceptive observation, no existence, and therefore no choice: for metaphysical 'reasoning' from notional
authority, whether human or assumed-divine, is as false and
unconnected as a dream.   If the related tie were not involuntary, but a choice by some voluntary agency in the brain, the
works of science, and indeed of the higher poetical intellect,

being uncontroled by Nature, would from the variable tendency of a supposed self-will in thought, be widely different from their present respective accuracy, order, and inventive beauty. For as science and the higher poetry represent Nature; when Nature presents to them her images of things, she does it by the necessity of her Law of the intellectual and involuntary tie. If the brain has a power of selecting its images, and of joining them for its free-will purposes, we would have confusion on most of the subjects of thought; and Government, Religion, Medicine, and Morals would present a stranger medley of irreconcilable notions than has heretofore confused all metaphysical and therefore impracticable Theories.

I have stated in another place, that when many images rise on a subject of inquiry, they have various degrees of relation to each other; what we have called the strictly Related tie, or a conclusion upon it, produces the truth of science, the rules of grandeur and beauty in the higher poetry, and in the esthetic arts; the other relations, under their different degrees, creating no strict perception of truth, yet sometimes affording an illustration of it, and only furnishing the slightly connected images of the resemblances or contrasts of wit, the oddities of humor, and the distortions of drollery: showing the ground of a preceding remark, that ridicule, founded on these fainter relations, is no test of truth, though often in sophistry used against it. Otherwise it would be to oppose false or feebly related images to those of the strictly related tie. Now the theories of Metaphysics, from the Greek etymology of *Meta*, beyond, and *phusis*, nature, being on notions beyond the perception of the natural senses, are by some implicit belief on authority, or by some other perversion of the ordained working plan of the mind, made up of its slightly related images; and the same perversion leads the metaphysical theorist to believe, the confused or false, and feebly related images of his notions are produced by his own voluntary choice; which would be only a selfish way of searching for the truths of God and Nature. Let every individual have voluntary, self-willed or chosen thoughts, and employ them on this world, as they do on that which is to come, and there would be as much self-willed contradiction in the limited thoughts, and confounding hopes of man, as there would be on the subject of the weather, if left to the voluntary direction of agriculturists, sailors, sun-basking lazzaroni, and children who are humored in their fear of thunder-storms. Fortunately all thinking being under the involuntary tie, Nature has made this Prime Minister of her mental affairs, so far independent of what is called the Will, that when the mind is wise, upright, instructed, and fit for its purposes, its thoughts and actions will always follow the necessary Laws of Creation; leaving it to the false theories of metaphysical visionaries to mislead the weak and ignorant into the belief, they have a self-determining spiritual will of their own. But even the metaphysical like every mind is governed, in the feebler tie of its perverted perceptions, by an involuntary power; for though it may appear to act *freely* under its confusion of images, yet these, like the perverted, incoherent, and certainly not *chosen* images of a dream, are still subject to the involun-

tary tie, of the necessary Laws of the brain. If the tie of
thought and word were not involuntary; when an intelligent
reader with a supposed voluntary command over them, has
his memorial perceptions of Milton, Thomson, Cowper, or any
other eminent poet, why should he not *choose*, for he would
desire it, the like higher images of grandeur, grace, and
force of thought and word, and thus attempt to equal or excel
them? If he has images and words appropriate to this higher
work, Nature will direct the tie; she does not write the
poem, she only prompts the word or thought he has in memorial though-hidden store, yet cannot lay the hand of his
choosing will upon it: but with either scanty or abundant
memorial images, he cannot *choose* the application of them;
which under a free-will he would have the means of doing;
since he perceives in the higher Poet, the character of image
he requires in the case.

It is not to be supposed the Reader can receive the whole
meaning of this Preface; as it is only an abstract of a more
elementary explanation of the subject, and of its practical application, in another Work; he is therefore referred to the
'Natural History of the Intellect,' if interested to learn more
of its character and use than is here described.

In the following Rhymes, the Author has endeavored to
give examples of the involuntary relations of the strictly truthful
tie of word or thought; and of others less connected, by which
the images of humor, oddity, and exaggeration are necessarily
though faintly joined to each other.

There will be found in the Work referred to, particularly

a note of the fortieth Article, of the thirty-sixth section, eminent illustrations of this subject, in the minds of Bacon and Shakespeare; the one a physical philosopher, the other a Philosophical Poet. They never *sought* the tie of relation in thinking or in words. The necessary image and the verbal sign presented itself to them : to the former, with the stricter purpose of scientific truth; to the latter, in pictures of the grandeur and beauty of thought and language, together with the fainter ties of wit, humor, and drollery. And perhaps the ease with which their great intellectual works were accomplished may be a support to a belief of the involuntary action of physical thought in the brain. For this involuntary action, like the involuntary beating of the heart, and other involuntary actions of the body, is carried on without the least fatigue; since fatigue, as a final cause, is to be regarded only as Nature's warning, that what is called voluntary action should cease for the time; rest being altogether unnecessary to the involuntary thinking process of the brain; in the exercise of which, except under perplexity, fatigue is never felt. Nay, the strict, original, and productive use of its involuntary physical method not only gives increasing power to itself, but otherwise preventing the distracting doubts of metaphysical fiction, in their thousand nervous forms, and consequent diseases, may contribute with other physical causes, to the prolongation of human life. Whereas the attempt of the metaphysician, and other notional and useless mental laborer, to reach after related ties, in a supposed voluntary exertion, produces those inconclusive and *dementing* images, which per-

petual-motion fanatics, mammon-speculators, agitated religion-
ists, forlorn lovers, and political ambition-mongers, who labor
after notions to please themselves, sorely experience in what
they call mental fatigue or exhaustion; which passing into a
chaos of thought will be liable to terminate either in fatuity
or madness.

Thus while there is no wasting exertion or wearing away
of the mind in its involuntary or natural working plan if un-
attended by bodily disease; the metaphysician, on the other
hand, in his attempt to believe in what cannot be believed, is
worried into an incompetent debility which prevents his re-
ceiving the corrective means of truth, and destroys his capacity
for demonstrative knowledge.

The composition of the following Rhymes employed, variously, the strictly related tie in the images of its offered truth;
and the less connected and feebler relations, even to contrast,
and _dis_resemblance, in the extravagance of its drollery. The
Author's method in thinking and writing is, not to endeavor
to _think-up_ the related images and words, but to _wait_ in the
patience of reflection for the required tie; and if there is within
the mind the memorial image to form either the strictly related,
or the feeble tie, Nature, not voluntary thinking, will necessarily bring up the appropriate word or thought. Let not
the Reader suppose this waiting for Nature's promptings
would delay his Composition. Of two minds with like construction, that which waits and receives by the involuntary
tie will not only outstrip in time, but will surpass in excel-
lence, that which would work and hurry over what seems to

be its Will. For the involuntary tie saves time by furnishing its images without confusion. The work, so to call it, of the *Will*, if done at all, would be only a tedious time of disappointed and distracted search. Our mind like the rest of physical Creation is under the necessary Rule of God and Nature; let us not try to thwart that Rule, by the metaphysical attempt to take their Law of the intellect into our own fictional hand. Follow that Law and it will keep us right, as it does the mind of the sub-animal world. If man were cursed with Liberty of Thinking, he would bring over his mind, more than the inconsistency, folly, and disaster, its mere fictional assumption has already done in the application of his metaphysical theories, to the administration of Political Government.

The Author preferred the Anapestic rythmus, as the most appropriate to the character of the Rhymes, though, if not carelessly constructed, the most difficult of our several measures; requiring for its unbroken fluency, a greater attention in the adjustment of accent and quantity, than the usual forms of the Iambic, or Trochaic line. In the variable purpose of the Rhymes before us, this greater difficulty required a copious supply of memorial images, for the strictly related tie of their truth, both in thought and word; its humorous and odd hyperbole, drawing from no less an abundance, for the feebler fictional resemblances, unexpected contrasts, the exaggerated descriptions, and satiric images of its pastime and humble pretensions.

In whatever light this trifle may be regarded, not a single

thought or word was *sought* and *found* by the Author. The stricter tie that produced what he truly states, and the less related tie of mere analogy, fainter resemblance, contrast or contrariety, in its humorous illustrations, were all impressed into perceptions by the involuntary ties of the working plan of the mind, as the like ties are raised in the mind of others, from the highest to the lowest perceptive degree; leading to the inference that its boasted *profundity*, genius, and originality are no more than its recorded description, not of human productions, but of images involuntarily struck-up by Nature on the brain. Should this be true, compare the productive intellects thus formed, with those of trite and vulgar rotine, in appointed Royal ministers, voted Presidents, everyday Provosts, Professors, Lawyers, Doctors, and Mystic Theologians, who in pride and vanity, persuade themselves, their thoughts and words are the undirected choice of their Will.

These Rhymes may perhaps amuse those who are merrily disposed; and though they contain not one instance of personal satire or caricature, yet if even the charge of insignificance cannot save them from the sneers of those corporate combinations for money and notoriety, and of those 'vested rights' which so often inflict unpunished wrongs; we may perhaps find in these sneers some self-confessed instances of the truth of their application to fraud, extravagance, and folly, to the disasters of popularity and avarice, and to the precipitate thoughtlessness of the Country, by complaining individuals thus putting the cap of the convict, of the fool, of a mocked Liberty and Independence, or of a flying Mercury, on their own well fitted head.

Separated from the odd and satiric subjects of these Pages, though brought within their view, two eminent instances of Public virtue are so remarkable, they could not be referred to, and named, without that compliment to justice and wisdom, which it is to be feared their posterity will be too much interested in other things, to care for or remember.

PHILADELPHIA, *January* 18, 1869.

PERSONS OF THE DIALOGUE.

THE NARRATOR, who introduces the subject, denotes the interlocutors, and conducts the dialogue with his own occasional remarks.

FOGIE, a deceased and analytic observer and thinker, whose writings are read or related by one of his Friends.

GO-AHEAD, a representative of the American delusion of Something new, and of the rapidity of National Advancement to its own exhaustion: called also Progress, Onward, and Muddy-faced Brown-Stone.

STRAIGHTON-AND-SURE, called also Plainway, one of the Class of Fogies; and Reader or reporter of his Friend's rhymes.

THE READER, the same with Straighton, and Plainway; who reads or describes from his Friend's record.

The time surveyed; Past, Present, and Future.

(xiv)

RHYMES

OF CONTRAST

ON

WISDOM AND FOLLY.

———◦◦◦———

THE NARRATOR.

I REMEMBER a rule, when we boys played at 'Ghost,'
To put implicit faith in the boy that bragged most,
And agreeing together, if he should take fright,
We might run, his authority proving it right.
But the mind ruled by Truth rests the hope of its pen
On the Book of God's Works, not the visions of men;
Thus the Author, on Nature his only Faith pins
For his Truth joined with Humor; and here he begins.

Looking-back on the World through my remnant of years,
And withdrawing myself from its hopes and its fears,   10
Nor so blind to its blindness as not to make plain,
That its search for contentment is groping in vain;
Yet I keep a sly window to peep if it still
Wraps its life in its play-things, to humor its Will;
So I thought I would raise-up the sash and look out
Just to learn what this Dreamer's now dreaming about.

I perceived a strange motion, a riddle indeed,
For the faster it hastened the less was its speed,
But the suicide course of its 'go-ahead' plan,
Plainly told by its failure, the riddle was man.*   20

---

* A knowledge of the simple constituents and working plan of the physical mind has enabled the Author to perceive, measure, and record its process, as that of any other material construction. And he remembers that some involuntary tic having presented the image and word of the 'strange motion,' in the seventeenth line, he sought no further, but waiting a moment, an involuntary law brought up the image of a riddle; for in the relations of things, and consequently of their images on the brain, the contradictory words of a riddle are connected by analogy with the condition of strangeness. When the line was completed, he did not *seek* the related tic that followed it, but waiting a moment, it brought up, unwilled, the contradictory image of a motion being lessened by its haste, which under its double meaning, has the semblance of a verbal riddle. The nineteenth line carries-on the chain of related tics; for the contradictory condition of a life, gloomy toward suicide, under the brightness of its advancing hope keeps up the related image of the riddle; and the tic of the twentieth line bringing up the strange caprices, and inconsistencies in the character of man, gives him as its solution. This is an illustration of the involuntary tie between four successive images in the working plan of the mind.

In following this exemplification, the Reader must entirely throw aside the old metaphysical notion of his having a spiritual consciousness within his brain, that distinctly from its organization calls up its related images, and informs him what the mind is doing: which immaterial agency is no more predicable, or to be assumed of the mind, than it is of a vegetable root having the entity of a vital principle to perceive the leaf it produces, or the mineral a consciousness to tell it of its crystalization.

I said in the Preface, that when the mind, discarding metaphysical or transcendental thought, employs the strict physical method, it is always done without fatigue. In ignorance of this, some grave Conformist to the sober follies, and errors surrounding him, may here say, the Author must have given himself much trouble with these silly Rhymes. On the contrary, they were brought before him by the bountiful and creative ties of Nature; and if not his duty it certainly was the turn of his pen to lay them before others. And be assured, Master Antijoke, grave or sour as you may be, you have more trouble, and no less silliness, under one hour of your queries and doubts, in keeping-up with the world's

Though the thing was an oddity, hard to describe,
Still it carried the marks of its changeable tribe ;
For while varied by species, by purpose and name,
They've a back-bone of Folly to shape them the same,
And if measured in motion, they'd seem not unlike
To that keen water hawk, quick ahead darting pike ;
But a pike's sometimes quiet, preparing to dart,
While a human fast-onward can't stop for a start.
Thus our Pike of a man was a queer-looking fish,
With the cap on of gay Fortunatus to wish ;   30
And he wished to do everything faster than fast,
Passing by his own speed with some new speed at last ;
Then he wished for Law-Logic, that by it he might
Quibble truth to be error, and wrong to be right ;
And for progress in knowledge is ready to show
If you don't learn in no time, you'd better not know ;

---

mystical opinions, and conventional though somber fashions, than the
Author of these plain truths in holiday and grotesk dresses would experience, if their continuation could be interminable. The use of the
mind, ordained by God and Nature, has no more tendency to debility, exhaustion, or insanity, than that of the undomesticated sub-animal, which
cannot be demented by scholastic fictions, nor terrified by metaphysical
Ghosts. Affording a striking contrast of the simple and easy material
method of the mind, with the conjectural work of the spiritualist, and
his notions ; therein being obliged to endure the thought-bearing exhaus-
tions of his 'profound' but unproductive investigations.

By the rule of the working plan of the involuntary tie, here exempli-
fied, every succeeding line might be explained. For though the Author
recollects the detail of the process, only in particular places, yet the tie
of images was throughout, the actual chain of Nature ; and being so ordained, an analysis of its connected memorials would show the forming
of its successive links. Writers who have been in the habit of regarding
their 'association of ideas,' will be able to trace the train of thought
in the Text ; and the Author may occasionally notice the stricter tie of
what he offers as truth, and other degrees of the less related perceptions.

That the slow-wise are foolish, fast fools are the wise,
Even swan-white itself should seem black to your eyes;
Thus as proof of his taste in his 'something new' tricks,
He's now building a house with black joints to the bricks.   40
But enough of his doings; covered up, it is said
He has Kangaroo legs for swift jumping ahead;
And his dress fore and aft, was half black and half white,
To denote by the last a fleet rival of light,
While his back's sooty cloth seemed to say he designed
In contempt to set slow somber wisdom behind.
Seeing now what he was, nor forgetting the rule,
If you know how to tap, you can draw from a fool,
I determined to make his acquaintance at once,
To draw froth, if no more, from this swallow-winged dunce.   50
May I ask, sir, your name? HUMAN PROGRESS, said he.
Oh, I've watched your Progression, and do you not see?
It's like Royalty's bit for its subjects to chew,
That instead of the Throne, they may gnaw 'something new;'
And as Kings amuse turbulent idlers with shows,
So your progress serves knaves, to lead fools by the nose.
For go fast as you can, and though faster your race,
Truth and Nature'll not give up the slow-and-sure pace.
Yet you sweep-up opinions the chaff of the times,
Can't you find a few grains, to support my poor rhymes?   60
Then I ask, Master Progress, who's he that disputes
The fast go-ahead strides of your twenty-league boots?
And to which you return in hyperbole joke,
That a snail in a hurry'd outrun the slow Poke;
While it's said, if he stops near your children at play,
They call, Here you old daddy, get out of the way.
Being anxious to know it, can you tell me who
Is this jest-word to some, and the child's Bugaboo?

Why, you don't know old Fogie? said he in surprise,
With his bald shaking head, and his half asleep eyes,   70
His pale fears counting dangers, his fingers expense,
And his mouth full of that vulgar thing common sense,
Taking look-ahead steps, with his cat-feeling shoes,
In a Prophet-cut coat, handed down from the Jews?
He's an obstinate pull-back old Fellow, and would
Make the world of fast nations stand still if he could;
But to judge for yourself, there's a Fogie close by,
Yet as near as he lives, I don't know him, not I.
There's his plain-looking dwelling, not Brown stone you see,
And he's plain altogether, as Fogies should be;   80
Still, except what I've said, he's a good sort of man,
To do nothing and die, for it's all that he can.

Disregarding what tongue-running Progress had said,
As he'd then 'something new' whirling round in his head;
And believing, from all his wild national schemes,
To make paper pay gold, upon Treasury dreams,
With an often-tried plan to get rid of Taxation,
By short-cut, in cutting the throat of the Nation,
That sketching his picture, he drew in mistake,
A young blind running fool, for slow wisdom awake.   90
'Tis a maxim, do nothing too much; as you'll find,
All your surplus is waste both of muscle and mind;
And it so came to pass, with our glib Go-ahead,
For his tongue ran so fast, I lost half that he said.
Then I called, as he passed, Onward's near and plain neighbor,
In Form and in Face showing hand and thought labor,
His house no political gift for sleeve laughter,
Like charity given, with hopes on hereafter,
Nor Plate, so received by like underhand bond,
Nor yet struck out of nothing by credit's frail wand.   100

Much too wary to fall under mortgage or lien,
And a foresight for sly money foxes too keen,
Free from care, full of years, of contentment and health,
Things unknown in card-houses of paper-built wealth,
Without debt, and no stay when his taxes are due,
And a heart for untrumpeted charity too,
Over-honest for office, or what's near akin,
If the knaves get possession they'll not let him in ;
Armed against all the credulous tricks of the day,
To make shadows of things with their substance away.   110
For it's wisdom's keen thought, and her strength at command
Give the meant Argus eye, and Briarean hand.

    I remarked, your address, sir, is STRAIGHTON-AND-SURE,
Since I've seen it as oft as I've passed by your door ;
Mr. Straighton, then tell me, have you ever heard
Of F, ó, G, I, É, not to speak the full word ?
For as Mammon is eating out knowledge, look well,
That our schools have some scraps left, to teach us to spell.
Long I've known him, said Straighton, his rules I was taught,
But he's sneered at by fools, doing things without thought; 120
He's the Prince of protection, for he alone saves
Those who heed him, from blind but still go-ahead knaves.
There's no time in which justice and truth have prevailed,
When the wise Fogie-Father 'as not always been hailed ;
Yet they give him hard names, as if years were a crime,
With his wholesome reproofs on the myths of the time.
But I'll cite a few cases, for others, not you,
To be told what old Fogies have done, and may do.*

---

    * The preceding description of Progress, Fogie, and Straighton, con-
tains various degrees of the related tie. That of Straighton by the Nar-

As the Savage so early, you'll first find him then,
One of Nature's wise Sachems, not voted by men,　　130
Rising Chief in his pride, from his self-teaching school,
That the mind seeing furthest, has God's right to rule,
With an age-tempered energy, stern to command,
By his own self-example, in heart and in hand.

　See in States more advanced, the great Sachem as sage,
Stored with knowledge, to use with the prudence of age ;
While the ignorant mind, in contrasted surprise,
'Tween the Sage and itself, raised the Sage to the skies.
Thus a weak superstition, without its conceit,
Kept in earlier ages its modest retreat;　　140
Now the fools their stark folly more plainly to prove,
Put the Fogies below them instead of above.
Yet we'll overlook that, for they did it stone-blind,
Set themselves before wisdom, in place of behind.

---

rator, and of Fogie by Straighton, the relations of truth. That of Progress
by the Narrator, and of Fogie by Progress contain the fainter analogies
of humor and oddity, even to extravagance and absurdity; of which we
have an example in the eighteenth line, where however, the tie takes
place between the words faster, hastened, less and speed. For faster and
hastened tied by contrariety to lessening the speed, the more impressive
action of the former, deceives or confuses the mind to the contradiction;
and it is passed over rather with the pleasure of an unexpected oddity,
than with disappointment at a false description. The like instances occur
in Transcendental Poets: as the following from Milton:

> The other shape,
> If shape it might be called that shape had none
> Distinguishable in member joint or limb.

Where the absurdity is reconciled to thought, by the tie between the
words shape used on each side of the proposition.

Unaware see the Sage, by a soothsayer caught,
Precious wisdom with trick, that foul mixture of thought;
But with Fogie's excuse, sadly true to the letter,
That nine out of ten would accept of no better,
He dropped for the poison of falsehood they quaffed,
A small portion of antidote truth in the draught.   150

On the list, Roman Senators gravely come next,
The old Fathers whom Rome's rowdy rabble perplexed,
With the Tribune's demand for Agrarian Rights;
By the Gracchi led on, those two speech-errant Knights,
Who so avarice-mad for their land-selling Laws,
That they both met their fate through their land-jobbing cause.
And with all the Last Fogie old Cato could do,
They gave Cæsar the crown, to get-up 'something new.'
Thus it has been with vanity, is, and will be,
When it sees its bright self nothing else can it see.   160
From its cry of fast onward, who'll save us, alack!
For as shouting flies forward, the country runs back.

We have heard of some Fogies, the Prophets of old,
Who oft tried to bring back Jewish sheep to the fold.
But sly Satan who wolves in sheep's clothing employed,
Not approving the sanctity Fogies enjoyed,
Laid their heads both together to make a fell sweep,
And while Nick stoned the Prophets, the wolves tore the sheep.
Yet a Fogie would sometimes, as holy words say,
Get the whip-hand of Satan, as happened one day;   170
When a flock of young Jew-lings, just let out of school,
Saw Elisha pass-by whom they took for a fool,
And like saucy-box children, in all forty-two,
Shouted, Go up, thou Bald-head, why, what can you do?

Some old Fogies do wonders, the bears told them that,
For of Maa's Hebrew darlings, they killed every brat.*

Other instances PLAINWAY thought useless to note,
Satisfied the above few examples to quote;
But remarked, I hold here, this small volume in trust;
The sad gift of a Fogie, gone down to the dust.   180
'Tis a book of reflections on persons and times,
Which my wise ancient friend has left written in rhymes;
You may read it whenever you'd feel indignation
At Fools who forget to remain in their station.

Now muddy-faced Brown-stone tricked-out for the day,
Stylish house, dashing equipage mocking display,
Having something quite new overloading his walls,
In a broken-back, top-heavy roof against squalls,
Yet within *hodgy-podgy* for fashion's odd pride;
And his Front filigreed like a cake for a bride,   190
I would try if he might, in some whirl of his brains,
Think of Fogie's Brick-house, and his small window panes,
With themselves too contrasted, no less in the kind
Of their dwellings outside, and their indwelling mind.
So I called out to Progress, pray stop if you can,
And hear 'something quite new' to you, on a new plan;
To prepare you however, you should know at least,
'Tis the work of a Fogie, not long since deceased,
Still if now for reflection too hurried, you might,
If you ever find rest, then perhaps find it right.   200

---

* Of the five subjects of reflection given in the preceding Text by
Straighton, the first four are founded on the stricter tie of historic truth,
and on inference; the last on the fainter relations of humorous analogy.

Oh it's all one, says PROGRESS, we'd not the less thrive,
Were the Old Men's Asylums to swarm like a hive;
But if true as you say, the old gentleman's gone,
He can do us no harm; then we'll hear, hasten on.
On the word I begged PLAINWAY to read or relate
What his friend, in the record had wisely to state;
He consented, and as he described it or read,
Take his words, for we give them as truly as said.

In a Preface, the Fogie tells how he was born,
All unknown, at the world's 'little end of the horn,'   210
Yet while knowing himself, not in vision so dim,
As to not see the world, when the world ignored him;
Setting forth that he came shortly after the birth
Of the greatest Republican Baby on earth,
And perhaps too the last, for its Liberty-Mother,
From SAM'S naughty ways, vows she'll ne'er have another.
The folly and vice of this Prodigy State,
Here the Fogie's choice Chronicles plainly relate.*

---

* From the wide influence of the involuntary tie, through all its degrees, in the working plan of the mind, whether on thought or word;
and from there being some analogy between all its degrees, it follows
that the stricter and the fainter relations are necessarily mingled in
human thought; and therefore it is more from convention than Nature,
that the marked distinction between the serious and the gay is regarded
in dignified composition; for truth might be, and often is, usefully illustrated by the fainter ties of wit and humor. Thus throughout the following ludicrous account of the Federal constitution, there occurs a succession of more or less related thoughts, from the stricter tie of truth, to the
slightest analogy in images of exaggeration, apparent contrariety, and
seeming absurdity; for there is in the fainter analogy of the Soap-Bubbles, a tie with the image of the inflated and momentary existence of
much of the glory, popularity, and conceit of mankind.

They began to *re*-tune their Colonial harp,
With its Thirteen old strings, some too flat, or too sharp ;   220
But the discord from 'nigger' notes proved so untrue,
That *E pluribus unum* of thirteen made two ;
And my life, with still more than it's worth, to a penny,
Our wrangling *State Rights*, out of one will make many.

When man in God's image, at first was created,
Still, whether in body or soul, is not stated ;
Yet proving all equal ; for if it so be
That we all are like God, so alike then are we ;
Though on this we declared ourselves one and all equal,
' Self-evident truth' changed her mind in the sequel.   230
Not liking this humdrum Equality then,
But to have High and Low mixed with Rich and Poor men,
They resolved in Town-meeting, that cure for State ills,
Which like Quackery cure it may, sometimes it kills,
To send Thirteen Soap-Bubbles, fit emblems of Glory,
From Thirteen New States of new National Story,
Commissioned to draw from some Fountain of Fame,
The proud order of Rank that ennobles a name,
Joined with honor and wealth, the great prize of the race,
Where the Jockeys too oft wealth and honor disgrace.   240
So the great Plenipos, on their final congé
As Diplomatists took their Ethereal way.
The Committee of Bubbles rose straight to the Sun,
Who was fixed, though apparently on his round run.
When the Bubbles' chief Bubble his mission declared,
That he'd come to seek honor, yet still was prepared
To take honor adorned with his own golden beams,
For greatness and gold are our day and night dreams ;

Yet they both are together so prized in our land,
That we beg to have greatness with wealth at command,   250
And to quicken our quickness, we humbly would plead
To be told the strange cause of his go-ahead speed.
Said the Sun, as my power consists but in light,
I'll be happy to make all your intellects bright.
They replied, it is wealth joined with honor they sought,
And they cared very little how little the thought.
Still the Sun was in hopes, it would please them to take
Such a Charter of Rights, as might serve them to make
A Republican Model, so purified-pure, it
Would puzzle Old Nick purified to endure it,   260
From demagogues free, and from speech-worried Law,
That the like 'mong his Planets himself never saw.
While the Heavenly Host, Comets, Stars, Milky Way,
Long the wonder of man, at their night-piercing ray,
Would be lost to their place in Creation's old story,
Eclipsed by that blaze of Republican glory.
The Bubbles were taught in Diplomacy's school,
For to seem frank and yielding at first, is its rule ;
Yet of Sophistry's gifts, to beware it's as well,
As the inch that you offer may come back an ell ;   270
So they all shrunk respectfully, hoping the Sun
Would in kindness forgive the rude wrong they had done,
In declining his brightness, by which he designed,
His new Western-State Star should enlighten mankind.
But; alas for that But, a short undoing word,
Which annuls past admissions, the moment it's heard ;
But, remarked, the Committee of Bubbles had birth
In a Nation more wise than all Nations on Earth :
Yet it signified nothing to Sovereignty's state,
If Renown blows no trumpet before Wisdom's gate.   280

Then they bubbled good-by to the Sun, who replied,
Of that trumpet beware, 'tis a dangerous pride;
If you blow it too high, you'll grow giddy and fall,
And away go your trumpet, wealth, honor, and all.
I don't think it will do you much good, what I've said;
'Tis to ruin you run; if you will, go ahead.
Then he shone on the Moon, and bid them call upon her,
For having less light, she might have all the honor.

The Moon being Full, all the Bubbles combine,
To inhale their full too of her glorious Shine, 290
Since they thought of its value if brought to the Earth,
In all serious questions, no less than for mirth,
And that should Metaphysics and Moonshine die-out,
There'd be nothing but Truth! and no Falsehood and Doubt.
But the Moon having heard of their ' go-ahead ' schemes,
Setting intellect far behind fictional dreams,
Her Asylum for Lunatics straightway unlocks,
And to them made it free, in a wild dreaming box.
Yet to swell out their greatness, and save packing trouble,
Blew all with her horn into one monstrous Bubble; 300
Which, filled with what honor the Soapsuds would bear,
She sent back to the Earth, to grow still greater there.
Here they called a mass meeting from Georgia to Maine,
Of the Bubble and Box, the contents to explain.
When some Public cracked (?) speakers long known to the State,
Wishing still to be greater, because they were great,
Made the greatness within the great Bubble so proud,
That it burst, and with Froth, wide bespattered the crowd.
This explains why a Fool, when self-stung by conceit,
Bloats its atom of Froth, his ambition to mete. 310

To be great, to be greater, and head of affairs,
Is our 'White-House' ambition, clean down its back stairs;
To be greatest in wealth, and in honor by dodging,
The Country's soul, body, meat, 'washing, and lodging.'

　'Tis said, Wisdom's maxims are rarely all lost,
Though distorted from Truth, among foolish minds tossed;
Thus one thinking Soap-Bubble had never forgot,
But the Sun's counsel kept which the others had not,
And so proved to a Few the wise purpose of light,
They believed all the Sun said of intellect right;　　　　　320
While the twelve of thirteen, showed that parable which
Made the blind led by blind, both 'fall into the ditch.'

　Now if all we have said of the Mission is true,　　　　　.
We're a Moonshiny people in most that we do;
For a Free Commonwealth photographed by the Sun,
Would have been the like picture, eye ne'er looked upon:
But by *vote universal*, they called for the voice
Of the People, which means a *few Demagogues'* choice.
Yet by juggling with freedom, it so has turned out,
We've free schools, and free feet to run gadding about,　　　　　330
With a freedom in Church, and to make us more pious,
Instead of one Faith, many Sectaries to tie us.
Then voting a Chief; Senate prone to disputes;
And a Bench to stretch out Law and Time as it suits;
In a triple-hung balance, adjusted so nice,
That a small loss of virtue might sway it to vice;
For should each pull with contrary opposite weight,
It would make a true equipoise over the State.
Yet with no balance-wheel to let each check the other,
Take care of the beam, when they all pull together;　　　　　340

But President, Congress, and Bench leaned so far
As to weigh the same side, down to sad Civil war,
When these nice triple Balancers, saw one and all,
Mene-tekel-upharsin's dark words on the wall.

On the practical work of Republican sages,
We've Fogie's remarks, still preserved in his pages;
And taking his thoughts on Financial Affairs,
We will show you some wheat 'mong Congressional tares.*

---

* The United States *thought itself* obliged, after the Revolutionary War, to repudiate the circulating paper debt, contracted under it. And in delaying the payment of certain promissory certificates to its officers and men, for military service, did acknowledge its obligation, though then unable to discharge it. The postponement lessened the hopes of liquidation; and as these certificates were sold by the needy officers and men, their value diminished in the market. Thus they became the stock-in-trade of the merciless Brokers. After the speculating *Bears* had beat them down to the lowest prices, and bought them, they used every means of influence on the Treasury, and on Congress, to create a Funded Debt, to the full amount of the Certificates, which had now passed from the Soldiers' hands into theirs. James Madison, of Virginia, then in Congress, with others, plead strongly but in vain, for the Soldiers, and in vain against what was called by its indignant opponents, the swindling Funding System. Mr. Madison, the Fourth of the Eminent Presidents, was in those days called a Gentleman, a political individual now hardly to be found; for he lived before the raging rule of the American Dogstar, with its insatiable canine appetite for popular notoriety, and an excess of a temporary Paper Money. Simon Snyder was Governor of Pennsylvania, and vetoed a Bill for Chartering Forty Banks, upon objections wisely foreseeing the enormities of a baseless Currency. But the avaricious conscience of the Banks defeated his veto, by two-thirds of the Legislature; and had it been necessary, they could have afforded to procure a larger majority of the Honorable members. Simon Snyder in aristocratic phrase, but in our Democracy let that pass, *was not* a Gentleman. We however, desire to speak of him here, as one whose memory is entitled to the highest respect, from his possessing a Chief Magistrate's Saving Grace of Truth and Honesty, and being thus more of a Gentleman than the greater part of his political successors.

How then came the first step on America's part,
To be falsely awry both in head and in heart ?   350
And in spite of foreboding, by old Fogie croakers,
The officers' claim found its way to the Brokers,
Whose funded debt fraud worked so cruel to cheat
The poor Soldier who marched with unshod bloody feet.
For the *Bears* ruthless tore the last shirt from his back ;
When the *Bulls* caught it up, and with cloven foot track
Knowing well the right ground for its scouring and bleaching,
With Treasury winks, and a Congress o'erreaching,
The shirt, by a neat financiering mutation,
Appeared on the rich Ruffled Rogues of the nation.   360
Though these may be gone, they've descendants who show
Some small bits of the shirt, which perhaps they don't know.
We had pleas for the Soldier both warm and sincere ;
What is that, to buy cheap, to lay up, and sell dear ?
For a bonus on profits with oaths sealed secure,
Never fails to make voting majorities sure,
If you call that thing sure, you can't trust very long,
And if chance makes it right, equal chance makes it wrong.
And though Madison plead, and urged equity's laws,
The poor soldier was starved for the vulture's gold jaws.   370
Don't believe, young Republic, that right can be fooled,
Or the order of things not by justice be ruled,
For the Works, not the Word of God's wisdom and might,
Antidote every wrong, in the end, with its right.
Though atrocious old Rome long triumphantly passed,
In her ruin Atilla brought vengeance at last.
Recollect your first sin, and prepare for the rod
Of some sure and retributive new ' Scourge of God,'
Who indignant at wrong, while his sword sternly waves
O'er the tribe of like Funded certificate knaves,   380

May in using that sword the like frauds to avert,
Give the watch-word, 'Remember the Soldier's last shirt.'
They had then moral Prophets unheeded alas,
Who foresaw what has since, and will yet come to pass,
That a National life with so bad a beginning,
Its moment of birth being that of its sinning,
Would swell the first frauds of its leading-string years,
To the crowd of impostures, as now it appears,
In coal mountain, earth oil, multicaulis cocoon,
Paper see-saw with gold, to the Bull and Bear tune,   390
With a still stretching road, for the Steam-horse to pant-on
Through snows to Francisco, clear over to Canton.
Since whims without weight of a stock-jobber's notion,
May tempt him to lay a rail-track on the ocean,
To dupe Uncle Sam, who with gaping-purse waits
For the Tea-trade of Europe to pass through his States.
Had the new Federal Ship, launched with hope and with pride,
On the high seas of honor triumphant to ride,
Not, alas, sprung a leak in her honor so quick,
And her Compass been Wisdom, instead of Gold Trick;   400
All had now been secure, to the Pilot the thanks,
Safe from wide paper Floods, and from wealth-wrecking Banks.
If the thieves had not snatched from the soldier's weak hand,
Or the Treasury paid *by its word*, on demand,
We'd have gone safer far, sailing under the banner
Of Gentleman James, and wise Simon the Tanner.*

---

* This long Note is properly an appendage to line three hundred and
sixty-eight, but there introduced would break the direct connection of the
topic; it is therefore placed at its end.

The effective character of a majority seems not to have been analyti-
cally set before us: though mankind are constantly called upon, either
as individuals or Communities, to act under its authority. If the Reader
has thought inquisitively on this subject, and has the same perception as

Look close to the seats of your Lawgivers' Hall,
If they draw not a '*Bonus*' they've pay and that's all;   '
See in Rail-Roads' Masked Monarchy, Banks viler still,
That in muffled-up darkness do just as they will;   410

---

the Author, he may pass by this Note. If he has not, he may here perceive a new manner of regarding it.

Majority has, with a doubtful claim to right and justice, always been
a despot, within the limit of his Rule; while his sworn enemy minority
lies crouching, sometimes barking out a feeble protest; for minority
never gains his purpose, till he in turn becomes the tyrant. Majority
was the first-born after three among men; for the sub-animals need not
its authority; the physical power of Nature governs them, as yet un-
humanized. He is as old as the time of Cain, when his father and mother
turned him out of Paradise, for slaying his brother, or, Geologically, as
the first three of Lord Monboddo's Gorillas, when they took up the form
of human government. Unlike our Fogies however, he does not seem to
have increased his knowledge or sagacity; a majority of five hundred
thousand in a Presidential election being no more effective, in their respective power, than that of Adam and Eve's one vote over Cain; or a
majority among three of Lord Monboddo's monkeys. Nor does age add
to his overbalancing weight; the one vote of Paradise, or of the forest
of Africa, giving a decision as conclusive as that of the Ecclesiastical
Councils of the early Christian Centuries, which *voted* Platonic dogmas
to be true; and sealed the tyrannical authority of an implicit belief, perhaps by the overbalance of a single voice.

From the state of confusion and dispute in which man is kept, by
ignorance of the structure and working plan of his own mind, and consequently of the mind of others; and which prevents his perceiving the
simple causes of the differences between truth and fiction, he cannot be
brought to what may be called individual unanimity, but remains so self-
contradictory, that not one in ten, except under physical science, is found
to think by the same intellectual principles. If the mind could be brought
to a knowledge of itself, it would perceive the purpose, manner, and means
of a self-unanimity, and would do everything according to its ordination; as the sub-animal in the unanimity of its self-government does everything aright. It will be here said, the sub-animal knows not its own
mind, yet properly follows its own purposes. True; but this knowledge
is, at present, necessary to the human intellect, for it alone of all animal
minds has metaphysical notions to turn it from its unerring physical instinct. A wise, observant, and reflective mind has a self-unanimity; and
its Primary, Memorial, Joint, Conclusive, and Verbal Constituents, as I

See the grasping monopolies, which at their pleasure
Seize other men's dues, and then waste without measure,
Rag credit that can't keep the wolf from the door,
To begin, cheats itself, and then swindles the poor,

---

have elsewhere called, and described them, act with successive and connected influence on each other, in their intended purpose, and perform it well. A fool wants this order and connection of his constituents, and acts evilly and wrong. Until therefore, mankind are brought to this general consent, in knowing the working plan of thought, for wrong thinking is never unanimous, they will continue to be unsteady, contradictory, and contentious, as individuals, and as a community altogether unable to govern themselves.

It is from an instinctive groping after a uniform mode of perception, that the greater number of Nations have looked for this desired unanimity, in the supposed mental system of a Monarch. He may have more power, for power is sometimes the energy of passion; but the intellectual fate of a King, with his surroundings of wealth, adulation, vanity, pride, ambition, and glory, resembles that of an obscure individual conspicuously and unexpectedly raised to our Presidency; one being born, the other voted, to his incompetence. This altogether perverts the natural order and balance of the constituents, necessary for mental unanimity, and leaves the subjects and the people, to the sole use of the forceful substitute for knowledge and truth, a numerical majority. Majority may then be rightly defined, to be that doubtful and blundering pretense to wisdom, sometimes right, but by its remove from a perceptive unanimity, oftener wrong: yet necessarily adopted as the only means for effecting the united action, though not as the unthinking believe it to be, the united intelligence of man.

In the common use of the word majority, it has become so identified with the terms power, knowledge, wisdom, and right, that to have a majority is seemingly to hold these instruments at command: and the responsibility of using them, which would be felt by an individual, is by a numerical preponderance, unacknowledged, evaded or forgotten, and its weight directed only for preserving or increasing itself.

There has been a vain hope to find the unanimity of a broadly instructed intellect, in the supposed power of wisdom and right, by extending a majority to two-thirds, or four-fifths, or to the undivided verdict of a Jury. The essential vice however, of a majority lies in its heterogeneous numbers; and their increase may only extend the power of the error or the wrong. The truth of a majority is therefore to be looked upon as a metaphysical notion, and phrase, not embraced by the purpose or lan-

3

Stock and branch then all these, if not from the same root,
Of that Funded Debt *Upas*, still bear its death-fruit.
Through our land had that poison-tree not spread so wide
Or success crowned Old Fogie on honesty's side,
We'd have had fewer perils, in pride be it spoken,
Still fewer Banks, Laws, and still fewer oaths broken,   420
Few Treasuries robbed, far less murder-blood spilled,
Prisons empty by *Pardons*, that ought to be filled,
Yet more Gallows-wood framed, to let something hang to it,
More Jack Ketches ready for justice to do it.

Enough now of wealth, gained by black and white lies,
Which has never yet made the world happy or wise;
Let us come to our harmless excitement and jokes,
That are every day making such fools of the folks;
As Processions, where each has his own self-delight,
Thinking all eyes on *him*, in his vanity's right;   430
And then mass-meeting mobs, ruled by Demagogue laws,
To fool-flatter that mob, and be paid by huzzās;
'Make-believe looking' soldiers, to show-off their 'Bosses,'
With trumpets and drums, to scare city work-horses;

---

guage of Nature; and as entirely beyond the reach of accuracy; like the
notional attempt to produce a human perception of the beginning and
end of Infinity; the existence of a substratum in matter; or of the enormous absurdity of a spiritual mind. But we live in the times of credulity
on these four nonentities; yet without believing them possible, must
quietly rest amid millions who are persuaded, they can obtain truth
from a majority; and perceive things that cannot be perceived: waiting
patiently for the time, when the mind, knowing its own process of unanimity, may assimilate those minds that now differ only through ignorance of themselves.

Democracies are founded on the will of the majority. Their support
then floats on uncertainty: no wonder they are self-conflictive, changeable, overloaded with despair, and kept from sinking at last, only by the
extended arm of some self-supporting and despotic power.

Law-breaking Show Fairs, once forbid by the State,
From their immoral ways, but evaded of late,
To raise Charity's tariff, with Robin Hood's lure
Of waylaying the Rich, to give *part* to the Poor.
Add to this, the Town Council, street idlers to please,
For a tax-wasting pastime hold popular keys,   440
Which right-turned on occasion, the secret explains
How the 'fuss' of excitement's turned loose on their brains;
Since there must be a movement for folly, fools say,
Or its wheels would stop short, and all fools pass-away.
Thus the streets seem curled into a main-spring for fun,
To keep-up Ninnyhammers all day on the run;
While such hubbubs so kill-off poor time with their pother,
One show finds itself wedged-up close to another.
Through Fools thus so jammed, if there can be found space
For a train to pass-by, without Foolery's face,   450
As the Fireman's Path, be the avenue made,
Showing usefulness joined to a yearly parade.

Yet you must not believe all Tom Fool's retinúe
In whatever the folly, to mere folly due;
'Tis some sap of ambition concealed in the root,
That produces the Show of its foolery fruit;
As, for all the sly underhand trouble to raise it,
Some honor or profit there must be that pays it;
And though folly's thousands huzzā in the field,
There's a few have their credit and wealth in the yield, 460
Since 'tis glory and gold ' get-up' all these Displays,
And without their manuvers, farewell Gala-days.
Thus poor broken-down Rome, as she drew to her close,
Having lost her ambition, had no need of Shows.
Still you'll say, that the Ignorant must be amused;
Very well, must they then be by folly confused?

Let them know the mind's structure, by which they'll be taught,
They've a mirror for Sights more amusing in thought;
Here they'll see God and Nature, in truth represented,
Not pictures of things as if things were demented,   470
But making their Shows out of knowledge, they'll find
The amusement they want is right-using the mind.
You can see even this in a Fool's self-content,
Satisfied for the moment, when on folly bent;
Thus a mind rich in knowledge, the sovereignty gains,
To be always self-happy, as Nature ordains;
With the world's writhing worm of ambition down-trod
To display in their truth, the unproud works of God.*

Stand aside for that multitude, hear all the noise
Of men black and white, dusty black and white boys,   480
With high City Dignities scrambling to hear
A new cut-and-dried speech from his Honor the Mayor;
So much music, such bells, and such prancing Light horse,
You would think of Boy Billy and Banbury Cross.
Not at all; 'tis some fifty Odd Fellows a-coming,
With aprons, belts, badges, their fifing and drumming;
A visiting movement, that ceaseless vibration,
The swing here and there of our pendulum Nation;
Some idlers of Gotham, packed off in Committee
To honor like fools of an odd Quaker City,   490
Whose spendthrifty Councils as 'Lords of Misrule,'
To pay Honor with waste, by the 'something new' school,
A magnificent Banquet resolved to provide,
For themselves, then their Guests, with friend-loafers beside,

---

* The succeeding lines in the Text, on Parades and Shows, have all the related ties, from that of the stricter truth, through their degrees of the diminishing analogies of ludicrous resemblance, contrariety, oddity, and exaggeration, to the apparent contradiction of absurdity.

By a stretching tax-conscience for thousands, or so,
To be Even with Odd, and to then let him go.
On 'one side of the mouth' this was laughable ; still,
With their close-crowded Scaffolds, and packed Window-sill,
To look sad, there's another, for National Guests
To delude UNCLE SAM to some vain Foreign Pests,   500
Who for honor or profit, parade through the Land,
Taking Liberty's purse, not the cap, from her hand.
Add to this, sly political Natives who stay
Off abroad for a time, to be out of the way
Of commitment, so fatal as vote-workers know,
To return, and beat-up for a popular show.
Thus with Council-packed coaches, in sun and dust seated,
And doleful as if of their useless time cheated;
But still with an under-hid smile in their eye,
That the Dinner! the Dinner! would come by and by ;   510
For sharp-set City Fathers, self-feeding, take care
To provide a rich Feast, the chief seat for the Mayor.
City Feasts to the Feeders are always ' dog-cheap,'
Where high gentleman spongers low company keep,
And to make all men equal, there's nothing, they say,
Like a ' cheek by jowl' seat at a free drunken 'spree,'
On champagne without cost, and none brisker or riper,
The head dancing round, while the tax pays the piper.

We're often called-on to waste time, and what's worse,
To lose money, called time, by a party Cut-purse,   520
For some demagogue pushed-on by favor or fraud,
To be puffed-up at home, to be smiled-at abroad;
With a Public Speech Banquet, for public applause,
Where the tongue lets out more than goes in by the jaws;

And the most squeamish appetite learns to digest
Rawest flattery's earfuls and not be oppressed.

  Over such British Follies, Peers stoop to preside,
As the Patrons of vanity, waving their pride ;
But in running-up State, or a stock-jobbing debt,
We're quite even with BULL, and may outrun him yet ;   530
For though JOHN is high-honored by Queen, Prince, and Lords,
We've 'his honor' the Mayor 'Running First' in his Wards.
Yet so wrapped-up is JOHN in his 'fuss-making' shows,
That he'll keep his bells ringing wherever he goes ;
And the Yankee, his progeny, still lacking brains,
Seems to prove the like foolery flows in his veins.
Then let vanity smirch its low honors; a Peer
Of the Realm should at least keep his Dignity clear.
But this sad Noble theme is too tender to touch-on,
For Blazon must read it 'Base Point' of their 'Scutcheon.   540

  When Moses commanded his Tribes to forbear
Image worship graved sinful from things everywhere,
Pharaoh's Egypt took fright, and by one sweeping order,
The impi'us old Fogie threw over the border.
Oh would, the devotion to wealth and to praise,
UNCLE SAM'S vulgar Gods, could a like Fogie raise,
To give some bitter draught, drawn by chemical art,
And of both worshiped calves make us sick to the heart.
Yet it's much to be feared, Fogie do what he will,
That the double Idolatry'll cleave to us still;   550
And instead of an inkling for gold and for fame,
Things of use, when pursued without wasting or blame,
That the 'flesh-pots' we'll covet of wealth and applause,
Will be rag-paper money, and vulgar huzzàs.

For as money and fame are assisted by cunning,
They've instrument-fools on their services running.
But Fame sprung of wisdom, of virtue, and worth,
Has a claim to long life, by the right of its birth;
While a Popular Name, got by puffing and trick,
Like a rocket whirs-up, and falls dark like its stick.   560
So to magnify littleness, it must be shown
Through the mist of pretension, or else be not known.
As the Fata Morgana, enlarging and pliant,
By haze swells the man out to seem like a giant.

   We'd once a brave Captain, who met on the seas
A Commander as brave, nearing on the same breeze;
As the ships came up proudly, addressing his men,
We'll be soon side by side; to your duty, and then
If you bring down one mast, mind, *No Shouting*, but keep
To your guns, till you lay all the rest in the heap.   570
Let Decatur's brief words rule the resolute crew
Of our great Union Ship, with its mutinous Few,
Strike the Ringleaders down, the sore people's tongue pest,
And, no Shouting, in quiet demolish the rest.
So in all else you do, why not do it in quiet?
You'll do it much better, and lose much less by it,
In muscle and breath, and the mind treated thus,
Will work more at its ease, unentangled by 'fuss.'
But it's Shouting for everything, everywhere Shouting,
To kill a mad dog, or kill thoughts with your Spouting.   580
If lucky on 'Change, must you shout it aloud,
And run jingling your purse in the ears of the crowd?
When you marry your girls to, if pushed, Any Body,
To count wedding gifts, and be called Madame Shoddy;

Must Fashion's Flag tackle raise flaunting your daughter
Before you know all, of the Groom who has caught her?
Should he turn-out Scamp, the poor heart-broken bride
Recollects the gay knot wherewithal she was tied,
With herself and trousseau, the sole talk of the Town,
For a while, turning Gossip's weak wits upside down.   590
Yet the last and not least, for the satiric rod,
Kneeling down to her Parson, as if he were God.
Thus of old the Show Heifer, in sacrifice state,
Decked with garlands was led by the Priest to its fate.
Must you ape Dandy-fools when you 'get-up' a College?
And planning new dresses, instead of new knowledge,
Give Boys a square board on their skull-cap, to show it
Was cut from their Block of hard wood close below it.
To give LL.D. which may mean, who knows what?
As it's Latin, one half of the Givers do not,   600
Must you trumpet it out, if from foreign applause,
When we've home-demagogues such Quack Doctors of Laws?
If you catch a big flea, must the Naturalists meet
To your honor, and skip in parade through the street?
If you sail-off abroad, on a vanity trip,
Must you 'get-up' wharf speeches, and flags on the ship?
Coming back, must they greet you with music, and say
You're as empty, save gossip, as when puffed away?
For a 'something new' Show, should a President squint,
You've a torch-lamp procession to find what is in't,   610
And the lights are put out, when you learn or suppose,
He looked inward, to see a small speck on his nose.
But in this semicivilized hubbubing mirth,
Of receptions, and speeching, and what's of no worth,
We're like hens, for my figure, your pardon I beg,
That will cackle so, over a chickenless egg.

Still, on all these ambitions, in mind keep the rule,
If there's honor and profit, there's more of the fool.

Here then ONWARD begged PLAINWAY, to stop and admire
The wonderful ways of the Telegraph wire.   620
Once thieves, for of old every trade had its Gods,
Worshiped Mercury, Patron of fleetness and frauds ;
Now the thief robs and runs, but words flying like thought,
Let him go where he pleases, he's ' headed ' and caught ;
While to do modern errands, by land and by ocean,
Swift Mercury's wings are an old-fashioned notion.
For Go-ahead's course is so done in a wink,
That he'as not even time to see, hear, read, or think.

Of these quick Lightning-doings, here PLAINWAY replied
He had heard, but knew little of those who so ride.   630
Still he always took time to see, read, and reflect
On what perils a much slower speed might expect.
For we'll find these fast Idols set up to allure
From the true line of Wisdom, slow, cautious, and sure ;
While the worshipers, blinded to plain counting sense,
Buy their gain of time's speed, at time's monstrous expense ;
And you say time is money, then measure it so,
That as time is drawn out, equal profits may flow ;
For in cancelling figures and time it is plain,
That your profits and time will just equal remain.   640
After all then your scheme is at best but a chase
Who shall lose fewest moments, and then lose the race ;
But be sure, if some Fogie should ever engage,
To once balance the books of this fast-running age,
That its profits, compared with its promise to pay,
Have been carried by wheels, steam, and wires away.

See the wonders of Fate, to our happy age cast,
Time and space squeezed so close, they are both dead at last.*
Ah, thou stigmatized August, marked month of its date,
In the year eighteen hundred and fifty and eight;   650
When Atlantic's Great Rope threw its long lasso loop,
To inclose Queen and President, both as its dupe,
Making each Sovereign party to each send its word,
Though while neither was deaf, yet they neither one heard.

---

* The lines that follow in the Text allude to an attempt, by popular
uproar, to conceal, or assist the difficulty and extravagance of an under-
taking, in eighteen hundred and fifty-eight, to cross the Atlantic with an
Electric Cable. The attempt failed; and the shareholders had a worth-
less stock on their hands. The Lines merely record amusingly the kind
of show, and encouraging foolishness, by which a go-ahead People are
*mis*hurried, when a popular current is employed to carry an incautious
prudence to unthinking prodigality. But speculation is like a cat, hard
in dying; or like a child, on one fall, is up-again to take another; and
after five years, the Cable, with other funds, and somewhat less noise,
was again tried, and succeeded, but to what degree of its purpose, is a
secret. Probably it is on the same under-water shelf as the Thames
Tunnel; and about to be as useless: except the London Bridges, in one
case, should be swept away, and the European mails disused in the other.
Except also, for stock, monopolizing trade, and political purposes, im-
patient *Quid Nuncs*, and for catching thieves.
    That portion of the Rhymes relating to the Cable was written at the
time of its failure, for a poetical friend, having a ready perception of the
Ridiculous, who had lived in New York. Her death occurred before the
time for sending them. Within the last six months, the thoughts have
been extended and varied to their present form, on purpose to illustrate
by truthful description, or by satiric or humorous exaggeration, the use
of the involuntary tie of images, on the subject of the Cable, and other
excitements and excesses of the American people. Though the Stock
and Notoriety Jobbing in the Cable-case have been in a manner suc-
cessful on second trial, its previous failure is humorously recorded as
one of those useless examples which the world sees or hears of and forgets;
but which might especially inform our wonder-mongering fellow-citizens,
that when they bloat their pretensions with metaphysical calculations
and hopes, they will do least, and most, when they work by the physical,
quiet, and patient method of Nature and Truth.

For the Rope still maintains, it was sadly belied,
And if not by Stock-jobbing, by what else beside?
Oh then how, Honest Queen, could your Ministers sleep,
Without half an ear open, their vigils to keep?
Not to hear and deny, to the shareholder's shame,
The mean forgery uttered in Royalty's name?   660
But a President's honor on taking his seat,
Is trod-down by his Cabinet's foul cloven-feet;
And if so, it might serve any stock-broker's ends,
Whether cloven or clawed, to buy up Cable friends.
While our keen Secretaries, all taught, *Quid pro Quo*,
Might take part with the Rope, and give conscience ' the go;'
For a Demagogue's palm, by its itching denotes,
'Twould be tickled by stock, money promise, or votes.

   Only think! when the Cable was broken asunder,
They called its success a wise Providence wonder;   670
Not warned by their frauds on a high earthly Name,
With an unblushing impudence, senseless to shame,
They invaded pure Truth's bright Celestial abode,
To return with the falsified name of its God.
Thus unpunished the lie; yet the first to be caught
By a knavish manuver, are last to be taught.
So poor UNCLE SAM Goose, who thinks just with the mass,
And JOHN BULL, who is Daft by the very same class,
Whistled into the trap by the stockholders' call,
Lost their little plain sense, time, ships, money and all.   680
Gabbling SAM and Gruff JOHN, were you really so poor,
As to not keep one Fogie, your folly to cure?
Or if not quite a whole one, a half, or a fraction?
One gray lock alone would have saved your distraction;

Can Congress or Parliament cease to be blind
To the plain, if it's known, working way of the mind?
It will tell you that no metaphysical sleights
Will explain that great riddle, Political Rights;
You will learn too what truth is, and by it take care
That your Sovereigns may each be too wise for a snare.　　690
Come then, blow-off the smoke of your truth-blinding words,
And your joint mode of thinking by flocks and by herds,
Like the owl think alone, with your ears and your eyes,
And with talking fools 'round you, reflect and be wise.
Thus in turning old Fogies, with prudence you'll tell,
You can move slow and sure, and the cry'll be all's well.
Then let April learn wisdom, and August stand first
As the month of all fools, as it certainly must;
But remember it well, and to UNCLE SAM's glory,
As National wonder surpassing all story,　　700
He's frank to confess by contrition's wise rule,
That he was the *confoundedest* long Cable fool.

On the other side BULL rolled his eyes on the wire,
Roared nonsense, but wouldn't set London on fire.
Still inkling for honor when honor brings wealth,
Made a shadow of Rank for the stock-jobbers' pelf,
And created a Knight, as a proof, proof of what?
That the spark passed the sea, when the Cable did not.
But like Jonah's quick gourd, vain Manhattan, fast child,
Bloated head, any sense (?) and league boots running wild,　　710
At the Cable's first auction, resolved to outbid
All the fools of the world, and in faith, so she did.
For with UNCLE SAM's Cities vociferous vieing,
Manhattan's last bid brought her off colors flying.

For blindfold belief, now it's known well enough,
You must hoodwink all eyes by a newspaper puff;
With an implicit Faith must receive what you're told,
And see chalk as if cheese, and engraving as gold.
If you say, you have tried all in vain to perceive it,
You hear, that's the best reason why, to believe it;   720
All fools reason thus; and to name an enormity
Fools can't forgive, 'tis the want of conformity.
So, with a faith in advance of their hope,
They assumed they'd already their hand on the rope;
But to save disappointment, by proxy they'd show,
For the likeness at least, of the rope it might go.
Hence what signs everywhere of the Cable prevail,
Men wore long Chinese cues, one dog a spliced tail,
Little boys with their miniature capstans were seen,
Little girls jumped the rope on the Battery Green.   730
And it's winked, but the slanderous point to be parried,
Some stylish young ladies, about to be married,
On cords 'cross *Fifth Avenue* hung out their clothes,
Looking like a Rag Fair of their Paris Trousseaus;
And a style that an Empress turned from in despair,
All the Modistes of *Five Points* soon copied-out there;
While a Fishwife who lived near the Fly-market Docks
Dreamed all night of her having rope-ends of lank locks,
Then appeared like Medusa, to strike Doubters dead,
With a wig of Electrical Eels on her head.   740
See such coach-loads of Councilmen crowded so dense,
And with not a child's wheelbarrow freight of good sense;
Such electrical slang, and such nautical gabble,
Yet no Fogie's voice in the amateur rabble;
Such triumphs of nonsense, at once you'd have guessed
'Twas a fool's boast of something he never possessed;

Such a hubbub with bells, that you fairly would think
Belzebub and his Gotham'd got something to drink;
While a band of three hundred steam whistles combined
Frightened many stone deaf, others out of their mind.   750
And a Galopade Air made a Circus Troupe prance,
But gave eight polka school-girls St. Vitus's dance.
E'en the fish in the Hudson, from noise thought secure,
Have the ear-ache till now, spite of ' cold-water cure.'
Then such crackers by day and such rockets by night,
That the clocks never struck, and the stars went out quite
Till the great shipping City, in great Cable pride,
Stretched its mouth in a transport of wonder so wide,
That it swallowed the mountain of folly to show,
If we're bent upon wonders, how far we may go.   760
Thus the mountain, so swallowed, must certainly prove it,
Though hard to digest, Faith had power to move it.
Great City of Dreamers, then pardon the joke,
When it's said from your wonder you never awoke.
But by groping through sleep's crooked lanes in despair,
Turned your wits inside out to show foolishness there.
See Saint Tammany Hall crowded to its last story,
To count a full vote to this great day of glory;
Since Yankees pass anything set up for ballot,
If sauced with right words to the popular palate.   770
And taking all places, Manhattan's the Town
To puff emptiness up, and collapse wisdom down;
For by turning its brain topsy-turvy, it's able
To talk prudence down, and to talk up a Cable.
So Public School Folly the little boy teaches,
To make himself President, he must make speeches;
Or not quick in logic, or smooth in *bel-letter*,
Must hire slang-puffers, to speechify better.

They'd cracked (may be) speakers, from North, South, and
    West,
By our plural superlatives, each puffed as best;   780
Such a cackling of tongues was ne'er heard, and they say,
They got three hundred speeches, fresh laid on that day.
Thus the Manhattan Show outparaded parade,
And outstripped the whole world, as she does in her trade.
What was Troy's sad Night wrapped in flames, with alarms
Of distinct human cries, and confused clashing arms,
If compared to the flames of the great City Hall
With the yells of its Firemen, 'niggers,' and all ?
That was triumph, by danger and long patience won ;
This, an idle commotion, where nothing was done.   790

    Though we can't confer Knighthood we're itching to do it ;
So taking a name, we a stigma tack to it ;
Not S, I, R, sir, but three H, O, N, letters,
Implying some men are more worth than their Betters,
To Demagogues given by voting's short hand,
Making Titular Rank in a Democrat Land.
Yet this office-dubbed Heraldry's multiplied so,
And at best is but common, and oftentimes low,
That to not be an Hon, by some Place-branding curse,
One may chance to be better, and cannot be worse.   800
But the man of 'Three Letters,' a Roman would say,
Must have got to the Senate, by stealth in his day.*

---

   * The classical Reader of these lines might here give an explanatory
Note, stating that in the Latin language, the word *Fur* signified Thief;
and that with the progress of Roman refinement and corruption, the
thief was called a 'a man of three letters;' either from some play of the
ear, or more probably from the general increase of Peculators in Pro-
consulships, the Army, Navy, and Priesthood ; or from Pretenders hav-

To return, Empress Gotham, sham Empress at least, '
Called her Wrong, not Right Hons to a great Sausage Feast.

---

ing by favor seized positions in the Empire, to which they had no quali-
fied claim; as these were all alike considered thieves, or no better. For
it has been the practice of all Countries, when they run too fast 'ahead,'
or magnify themselves to Ruin, to modify the force of criminating, or
vituperative terms, on an increase of the vices or follies that deserve
them. There is indeed no instance, far as my limited reading extends,
to quote of the 'man of three letters,' on the above-stated principle; but
it may be inferred, that in Patrician intercourse, many a culprit has, in
modified phrase, been so called, when the 'good society' of a very rude
people would not bear the plain Latinity of thief. As on the detection
of a liar, by a wink between refinement and morality, he is said to be in
error; or when Members of Legislatures, and Councils or Lobby-Loafers
receive a bribe, it is said *professionally*, to be for 'Services rendered.'
And it is the same with all nations, whose civilization becomes bewild-
ered in purpose, forgetful of the reality of right, and of the name and
punishment of wrong; under restless excitement on the Rapids of pros-
perity, before the catastrophe of its fall. And this is the bustling and
confusing time, for the men of 'three letters' and of other ameliorative
titles.

A vigorous and honest nation speaks a plain meaning language; and
one who covertly takes your watch or your horse is plainly called a
thief. In a nation grown wildly extravagant, and covetous, when a like
depredator, through his office, robs a Custom house, or a Treasury, the
utmost his friends allow is, that he has committed a 'breach of trust;'
and if by compulsion he compounds the villany by restoring the plunder;
or by political influence obtains pardon of an Executive, he comes off
with the character of a disremembered defaulter, perhaps of a respectable
man; and good manners at least, if not the Law, require that no allu-
sion shall be made to his misfortune, under penalty of banishment from
'decent company;' or as a culprit, going to prison instead of the Robber.

Formerly, if a borrower from a bank was unable to repay, he was, as
a warning to lenders, properly advertised as a Bankrupt. Daring to do
this now, a just and independent Editor would be prosecuted for defama-
tion; while nine-tenths of the Jury, and of the Community, from compassion, which has usurped the place of Law, or from the chance of coming to the same condition of bankruptcy, would cry-out shame, on the
unfeeling exposure: as if enormity in mercantile disgrace is no more
than the accident of speculation; and the extreme of political turpitude,
only a subject for Party opinion and use.

Now, the Sausage was laid 'round a lengthened Park table,
And stuffed, near as could be, to seem like a cable;
But was to be looked at, not cut, under hope
That the omen might somehow keep cuts from the Rope.
Yet they ate-up all else, and drank deep to the Cord,
As the Ladies who witnessed the Spree bring us word;   810
Still, regarding the Rope and Their Hons half-seas-over,
The Girls, which was tightest, could never discover.

Since Ladies have come in the Boxes to sit,
Looking down on the men's drunken spree in the Pit,
To be toasted as 'Heaven's best gift,' with exceptions,
And served in their seats, with champagne and confections;
While 'strong-minded' women respond in their cause,
For a greeting with shouts, and smash-bottle applause;
It's perceived, after all that's of Lobby Gals said,
They sit back of the Spree, to be flattered and fed.   820
But a woman's ambition will wax while it lasts,
And as Gotham's High Dames are the fastest of Fasts,
They bethought, on this liberal day of 'rich' sights,
To set-forth their known Census-majority rights;
For as numbers still give in our Country the power,
It seemed very strange, that as up to this hour,
If counted by noses, the country would then
Show a few sneezers more, for the women than men,
Or to rate them alike, how the men should still claim,
To bestow on that Country the masculine name;   830
And with Yankee discoverers, real or sham,
Not to find a fit Help-mate for lone UNCLE SAM.
Then for Cabinet aid, not wife-like to dispute him,
We've frugal Aunt Nelly, who would perhaps suit him;

4

And 'spite of SAM's debt, and his legal rag-tender,
We think she might turn him from Spendthrift to Lender.
To save then our Lawyer and Broker Taxation,
Give SAM and Aunt Nelly the purse of the Nation.
So grant what we ask, and we promise you fair,
We'll not *yet* press our claim to the President's Chair.   840

This vain wish of their heart, if Fast women have any,
They gained by our governing rule of the many,
And told to the world, that by patience at last,
They had raised NELLY's Flag on the National Mast.
Then in Red, Blue, and White, two and two, miles of women,
Dispensing with Page-boys, to hold up their trimming,
Paraded the streets of the chief Yankee cities,
And Poets, all Hens, hatched their newspaper Ditties ;
While school-girls of Schuylkill's small vilage of Kelly,
All day rang their Bell, and made rhymes on AUNT NELLY.* 850

---

* Oh the Women! God bless them, as man will not, with a better
education, for perceiving with their senses, and comparing with their
thoughts, than that to which they have been wrongfully doomed. Since
they rank above the common masses, who would keep them in ignorance ; it is lovingly to be wished they could be expanded in breadth, and
efficacy of intellect, to be the *equal* half of the more improved and elevated portion of mankind. We have in another place, proposed the
revolutionary method of educating the mind to a knowledge of itself;
by which both women and men may be exalted to a lofty equality: but
to which the superannuated method of Conformity, in superficial and fictional instruction, has never aspired. Women are aiming at an elevated
state, without that knowledge of their own minds necessary to attain it.
They have therefore, in following their merely fluent, fictional, compil-
ing, and fashion-serving intelligence, not considered that all their
strength may be only self-confidence ; or if real, it may at last shake
down the pillars of their happiness. And let them beware lest the path
to their Rights, like that of the men's, may have thorns by the way-
side, and end in a labyrinth of contention among themselves.
   Having been misled by fanatics, and British Nobility, in joining the

This Episode closed, on the Fair of the Land,
The narration returns to its subject in hand,
Showing how to Manhattan's high honor installed,
A committee of twelve Burgomasters was called,

---

hue-and-cry for freeing slaves, in the manner it has lately been effected, and not looking even at the beginning of the mischief they are together doing; they are now playing the hazardous game of Liberty, as they call it, for themselves, without perceiving they may fall to a like condition with the negroes, in having no master; and a hope of contentment in freedom, too distant and confused to be comprehensible. What, except Education, which is a matter of their wishes, not of their rights, do women want, which they have not already, and now are fit for? By education, we do not mean the vaunted systems of puny Public Schools, incompetent Ladies' Seminaries, and private Aristocratic Tutorage; for in the wrong road, the wheelbarrow, carriage, and gilded Coach will never arrive at their destination. Have not women immunities and powers enough, when they are sought, and bowed down to for marriage? Yes, but this is an old-fashioned privilege; they want the 'something new,' of voting. Why to all its intents and effects, they do vote and rule, on the wide Benevolent question; vote themselves to all the seats in a Rail-car; have a patent-right to stand before a man at a Concert, and stare him out of his seat, without even a 'thank you;' are addressed first in an Assembly; and are the Tyrants over themselves in Fashion, the hardest of all forced or voluntary slavery. If they would take part in government beyond their present influence, and 'run for President,' they must begin like Lord Monboddo's monkeys, by dropping their cumbersome train of tail; enroll in the militia; be drafted in war; carry paper lanterns in night Processions through muddy streets, and scare the cats, with the novelty of *Soprano* huz*zees*. When some Fast Camilla-woman should come to the Presidency, by the majority of numbers, the first act of her sovereign arithmetic would be, to make a cypher of her husband. And here comes a 'secret of State.' To suit the Aristocratical Notions of our Republic, she would call herself Queen of the 'White House.' Another strong-minded Zenobia! But how would she address her now emeritus Lord and Master? When her voting subjects would have occasion, they would call him, 'Sneaking Consort' *ex* officio.

No, no, dear companions! This mockery of power may get you into puzzling realities. Your Rights are, to throw off your flimsy occupation of fictional thought, and fly-away fashion, and to put on the substantial and durable Robe of observation and reflection; and by knowing your own mind, you will learn how God and Nature have ordained you to use

And their English Rope-Mummers decreed on the spot,
The Slave-Freedom of Gotham, in, query in what?
A gold box to be sure; no, no, nó, her Imperial
'National Currency' scorns that material;
Since, Bank-aid conniving, they beat down its price,
And might pass for gold-beaters; yet all in a trice,   860
They so distance small-capital knave lag-behinders,
You'd think them by trade, filthy-lucre gold finders.
It's sheer broker-trick with rag-paper I'm told,
For though rogues heap gold riches, you never see gold.
So they chose what is made into treadmills and stocks,
Rather ominous that, for a Privilege-Box!
It was plated with Pinch-*back* the leaf very thin,
And by broken Bank promises papered within.
Still they voted their cheap wooden box an Ovation
With Holocaust rites, from a rope-zealous Nation;   870
For having outdone all the fools of the Wire,
To undo themselves, set their State House on fire.
Ah Gotham, next time, give the Fogie his sway
And perhaps he'll prevent such another hard day;

---

it. Then those who have always loved you, will turn their love to adoration; and the pride of deserving it, will listen to smooth-toned, but ruinous flattery no more.

Let men, every one for himself, wrangle about the metaphysical word Liberty; and ruin future, as they have their wasted and long forgotten Empires, by the besotted 'logic' of contradictory verbosity, on a term that cannot be defined, except by every individual for his own purpose. Do not join the interminable hunt after human freedom; Nature has taken a free Will from man, and made us slaves to her authority, to others, and to ourselves.

These things for your intellect. For a secondary essential, let your aristocratic Ladies play their Battledores, and shoddy girls skate their High-Dutch. If you have compact shoulders, rounded hips, straight limbs, with pretty hands and feet, exercise will fill up your figures, as calisthenic models, charming to look upon: but this should be no purpose of mine. Farewell.

Or if scourged e'er again for an August Show racket,
He'd not give his coat, for your new Gala Jacket.
Turn Croton from Wall Street, it can't wash relief,
From the Tombs keep your 'Social position' rich thief;
Let your 'High Fashion' rob without conscience or fear,
Both the Bank and the Custom House, year after year;   880
Then go winter in France; in the Spring coming back,
Try the same work again, on the very same track.
For if Paper SAM spendthrift, with millions in store,
Were to lose all his rags, he has plates to make more;
And as paper pays paper, it now is the trade
To make-up paper losses, by fresh paper made.
While the Banks and the Treasury, birds of a feather,
Not held by gold strings, will fly both off together:
And countless sums vanishing, no one tells where,
UNCLE SAM'S *nolle pros.* would make rogues and all square. 890
Then let Congress, Assemblies, and Town Councils still,
Throw off millions by millions, and tax at their Will;
For the Rogues may well plead, if you charge them with theft,
You've no money to steal, you have only Rags left.

In a field seven wise-men, three larks tried to fence,
But the larks soared and sung-out at man's want of sense.
Would you fence in our jail-birds, then let UNCLE SAM
Sew our bribe-pockets up, and case-harden our palm;
For though High-flying Knaves through jail roofs cannot soar,
They can pass pardon-free mercy's golden-hinged door;   900
And no keys are like two, in their value akin,
To keep law-breakers out, and unlock them if in.
'Twould be easier far, to fence close in our ships,
All our office thieves, forgers, scamps, idlers, and 'rips;'
Let them feel Gibbet Island, the Buccaneer spot,
Whereon Morgan, his mutinous crew left to rot;

And if counsel and Judge from their high duty fall,
Give them Judge Lynch's tree, most upright Judge of all ;
Thus in freighting off vice to be punished you'll find
That the Gallows does more than your Law left behind;   910
Use the Gallows in earnest, if that fail, go back,
For they don't mind quick choking, then try the old Rack.
But with justice unbribed, and no rogues left to lead it,
Your honor'll come back of itself when you need it.
Yet still you proceed on some new purpose led,
Not for thinking, as should be, but running ahead.
See your Clubs of Land Sharks, we call town-building plotters,
Alluring poor dupes, by some gentlemen Squatters,
By 'slang-whang' of Homestead still doubling and doubling,
With rest for old age, free from lawsuits and troubling ;   920
For know, clear as moonshine, then buy or you'll rue it,
That Town out of Town, will soon bring the Town to it.
There's wealth for your child, on that miserly plea,
You shall have it, my boy, when it's no use to me.
But beware of this money bait, spread on new lies,
'Tis your own way of poisoning honey for flies.*

Here the READER stopped short, in default of a word;
And as ONWARD himself had long wished to be heard,
He assumed this delay, to point out on his part,
What he thought would at once the old sleepy-head start,   930
And to plainly speak-out, in his own way of rhymes,
Some most wonderful truths of the go-ahead times.

---

* The preceding lines of the Text contain, by general consent, too
much of the stricter tie of truth, to admit by conventional propriety, the
fainter analogies of things, that might create a perception of the ludicrous; or if allowed, it would be under that treatment of an error, in
which we sometimes begin by laughing at Folly, and end in the corrective Wisdom of truth.

Now awake, Father Fogie, be rubbing your eyes,
Stretch the bend from your back and endeavor to rise,
Just to look-on the glories improvement has spread,
And you'll presently worship our God Go-ahead.
See Columbus returned in his chains as he died,
With meek Penn, in the straight Quaker coat of his pride;
But so shrunk in surprise at the prospect around
That the fetters and coat loosely drop to the ground.   940
Here's a progress in time, let past ages beat that,
With their Mercury, winged at his heels and his hat;
Macedonia's proud Butcher, did all things in slow time
Though marching to India and back, counted no time;
His wonderful horse too, that only kneeled down
To take vain Alick up, as show-off for the Crown;
But in these onward times we've a light-beating horse
Held all ready to start, by a Keeper called Morse;
Nature's wildest fleet steed, kneeling down to the Wire,
Which rubbed and let free has his nostrils of fire.   950
Yet crossing the Ocean, it's said as no fable,
His tail's still in one, when he'as reached t'other stable;
And grooms have declared, that right training his breed,
He'll at last beat himself by some miracle speed;
For with track 'round the world, over land and by tide,
Both his head and his tail will come in side by side.
See how Science advances; let old Fogie think,
We've more knowledge than means to record it in ink.
Hear Geology reading her Bible on stones,
And by quoting God's Book on some once living bones,   960
Has caught Genesis fibbing; and God's earthly pages
Have turned a few thousand to millions of ages.
While Schools glut the market, ambitious to try
How a hungry demand can be met by supply;

And itinerant Lecturers now let us know
What a distance, a small scrap of learning may go.

  See the Bookselling Progress to what it is brought,
Far before the old Fogie's slow working with thought.
A few copies of Shakespeare are now all we need,
Since the mass of the world such old trash never read;   970
While the Printers, oppressed by the mind's thinking fetters,
Make Books as they should be, ink, paper, and letters.
Still, not to regard what pretenders might say
That one Stevens and Aldus had done in their day,
Passing over dry classics by Wynkin de Word,
We've 'Tom's Cabin' by millions struck off for the herd;
And the same with 'implicit belief' in conjecture,
Cock-Lane's famous Ghost, and Lord Lyttelton's Specter.
While Novels and Newspapers, both well-designed
For the everyday appetite found in the mind;   980
Quite unlike the old books, full of thought and of truth,
That perplex us to death, with their knowledge uncouth,
You will see it's all right, by a go-ahead notion,
To keep useful thoughts in perpetual motion.

  Here PLAINWAY remarked, on these daily eternals,
Reviews, and newspapers, tracts, novels and journals,
You have Fogie's true scope of a people whose pride
Never thinks, but *outreads* all the nations beside.
Your distraction denotes little brains in your pate,
And such reading will bring back your Zoophyte state.   990

  ONWARD then took his turn, and proceeded to show,
Some strange things, he was sure that Straighton could not know.
I have heard children say, there was once a time when
Pigs were pigs, to squeal out for their food in their pen,

And the men were so slow that the swallow found rest
In the old Fogie's beard, to build safely its nest,
While the turkeys tobacco used strangely to eat ;
All which seems childish nonsense, too flat to repeat.
But we see 'twas for contrast to present improvement,
Since swallows can't now equal Go-ahead's movement ;   1000
And 'learned' pigs' progress have made them so smart,
It would puzzle the High School, to learn the pigs' art :
Strutting Gobblers taught speech, throw their quids to the rabble,
With millions of words for one former throat-gabble.
Yet still the same Law all advancement obeys ;
Years seem dwindled to months, and long months into days.
Once in traveling from daylight to evening, it took,
Leaving ' George and the Dragon,' to reach Powles-Hook.*

---

* In our early days, the 'St. George and Dragon' was a Tavern, at the Southwest corner of Second and Arch Streets, Philadelphia; from which the passenger Stages to New York began their route, which terminated at a mere Ferry House on Powles-Hook, now the site of Jersey City, the West side of the Hudson, where the passengers crossed. Sad Rail-Road havoc has been committed on the time of this hundred miles. Whether it will pay for the killing, as surely as it remunerates its stockholders, for a monopolizing and imperfect road, is not quite ascertained; yet we know one of its results, common to all our cheap locomotive traveling; that of accommodating, or prompting, or increasing, the home changing restlessness of the American People.

Unconstitutionally, we are a very Aristocratic People; and some of the class who acquire wealth, and cannot employ themselves, except in making more, or in some ostentatious and questionable munificence, may affect to imitate all the Court, and many of the highest Rank in England, who with unceasing change of visiting friendship or ceremony, so fly about, and are be-newspapered all over Britain. With us this gadding is a general idleness, for time abroad and at Home is about as twenty to one : and perhaps it may indicate the overruling prevalence of this affliction of vacancy, or 'mania erra (or vaga) bunda,' as Cullen names it, to quote the incontinent instance of our domestic Author of the endearing emphasis of ' Home Sweet Home;' who from whatever more worthy and alluring motive he left his Country, and remained abroad, could not find

Then you went slow and sure ; on my word I'll engage,
You'd read Milton half through, as you sat in the stage.   1010
Now, in darting that distance, poor time has no quarter,
For sandwich, nor e'en for a small glass of water :
Yet hunger's loud clamors to New York and back
Bring up Paddy's loud greeting each end of the Track.

See our boasted School System the Freeman's proud salt,
The Republican pickle, to cure every fault ;
And some deep metaphysical critic presages,
Our School-salted minds will keep wise through all ages.*

This outbreak of moonshine roused STRAIGHTON to say,
On the Public School Problem unsolved in our day,   1020
That with present and past calculation to rest-on,
'Twould take many millions to settle the question.
But Schools having don'd the Political coat,
Must remain as they are, a mere a, b, c, rote :
And if Onward could think, it would not take him long
To admit his School System half right and all wrong.
For the mass who to read, write, and cypher aspire,
To give them no mind, they will never look higher.

---

it in his heart, to stay and enjoy the delight of that 'no place like Home,'
which he so feelingly celebrates.

* All the remarks on the School and College system that follow in the
Text, are to be considered as founded on the strictly related tie of truth,
however they may vary from the pedagogue and professorial modes of
instruction. These in many departments were adopted at first, and
have been continued, on those fainter degrees of the relations of things,
which on subjects of less moment, and of more mystification, would produce the perception of oddity ; and may, as intellectual times improve
by the mind knowing itself, make the present *visionary methods* of opening it to a broader and more accurate range of thought, appear in contrast, to what it should and might be, only a slight remove from the
ridiculous.

Teach schools what the brain is; therein lies the source
Of the power to raise intellectual force.   1030
Not to know the mind's working plan, hopeless the plight,
To be ignorant when it works wrong or works right;
Thus the Councils will find their time-wasting High College,
May pay high for jobs, but can't purchase high knowledge;
This comes of Free Thoughts, then set free thoughts to teach,
They'll disclose far beyond what slave-thinking can reach.
You import English sparrows, as 'something new' toys,
To be killed by our gun-using, stone-throwing boys;
Can't you 'get-up' that new thing, time never has shown,
The mind knowing itself, to make other things known?   1040
Try free thinking in this, it will give you new senses,
And sweep from your mind metaphysic pretenses.
If this you can't do, keep your schools up till when,
For one million now wasted, you'll squander full ten;
They may chance-cure themselves, and as seemingly wise,
Make their evil so great, it may open your eyes.
But again, should your salt lose its savor, then what?
Though it's fresh for fools' tails, for wise heads it is not.
It can't pickle your officers proof against stealth,
Where each thief takes his share in a free Commonwealth; 1050
Since a kind of self-theft rules Republican States,
For the Government's theirs, and its taxable Rates;
Thus the People and Revenue passing for one,
'Tis not stealing in Office, when each takes his own.
And for bankruptcy, swindling, and such small enormity,
We'll not perceive them, through gen'ral conformity.
Happy dilemma! as free schools will show it,
Not curing corruption, at least we shàn't know it;
But statesmen, we're told, and long-head financiers,
The unsalted Free High School will furnish for years,   1060

Where the boys early learn such repugnance to work,
They'd be gentlemen, or at least some sort of clerk;
And abhorring trade labor as vulgar, they fall
Into Politics, lowest slave-workshop of all.
We are very pound-foolish, in building our schools,
Though not ha'penny-wise in the intellect's rules.
Try to find what the mind is, and that will unfold
A bright vista of wealth more enriching than gold.
Do not keep waste your garden, by Nature designed
For the growth of God's truth, not the weeds of the mind, 1070
Since the shortest crop reaped, from its physical field,
Will exceed all a non-thinking Spirit can yield.
Let alone paying jobs in your old art of schooling,
Mind can't serve you there, for it's no friend to fooling;
Let words strictly used teach the way to the brain,
Or your phrase 'mental culture' will nothing explain;
For it takes no more thought, as we teach, to express
One's own name with a cross, or write A. S. S.

Once monastic endowments, in Catholic days,
Helped the idle to fatten, by alms-cringing ways,   1080
Made the mendicants prosper in houses and lands,
Set the people to work, while they folded their hands;
Used the hypocrite's mask, and devotion's sly art,
To make dupes to the Cloister, in purse and in heart;
Seized two-thirds of the people's land under their feet,
And the rest took in tithes, their low vices to meet.
Turned Religion to indolence, mind into notions,
In sleeping or waking, to dream its devotions.
So our schools made for paupers, the Rich craving still,
Ask their alms, to save paying the old 'Quarter Bill.'   1090
After all then your schools, which are only mind-warpers,
Can't make paupers wise, but the Rich turn to paupers.

If schools spend their millions, to buy let it be
Virtue, knowledge, and truth, not alone a, b, c.
Teach your childen to think, which your teachers can not,
And their mind will be fit for the purpose of thought;
Leaving newspapers, novels, and such vacant reading,
That turn the mind back, or arrest its proceeding.
Learn what has passed-by, it may chance-make you wise,
As you'll see fact enough if you half use your eyes.　　1100
On your pilfered 'State Works,' so much borrowed and lost,
That you jumped to sell-out, at one-fifth of the cost.
But beware of the age, when the school-time may come,
Like the Convent, to eat up your house and your home,
Keep in mind well the warning of Church and of State,
Or the School and Controler'll be moths quite as great;
For the time may be near, when some king will arise
To assume your School-houses as royalty's prize;
By the Freeman's free rule, taking self-will for right,
As a forfeit to waste, claim your schools by his might.　　1110
And as Henry once seized on the Monks' lazy dens,
Seize your multiplied Brown Stones, slates, primers, and pens.
Then give up such instruction, and try in its place,
What will teach man his mind, and thus change his whole race.
If by a, b, c, system we strive to obtain
Honest voters and Presidents, 'twill be in vain;
And some power'll turn up, who'll ordain the best school,
For the wise to teach children, not fool to teach fool.*

---

* Our Public Charity Schools, like everything else in the Country, which unnecessary and thoughtless change can ruin, seem overgrowing to destruction, under the power of our vulgar Demon of Velocity and Accumulation. Our Utopian vision of Charity began with an imitation of a modest, useful, and permanent Parish School System. The Scotch having the sagacity to perceive, that if instruction, like every other cost-less favor, should be gratuitous to the ignorant, it would not be valued

Here then PLAINWAY demurred and regretted to say,
That some leaves of the record had faded away;   1120
And if Onward would listen, he would himself try
The dim leaves of the Author, in part to supply,

---

and might be abused. They therefore charged those who received the
benefit, an endurable part of the expense. But the money-loving Republic loosened the spasm on its heart, to be the model of liberality; and
about the time of the first slip of its justice, in giving its soldiers' pay to
the brokers, it generously prepared for opening Free Schools to any one
who would be so mean as not to lay up ten shillings from his speculating
extravagance, towards paying for his child's education. And now for
the primitive brick school, Go-ahead must have 'something new' of
muddy brown stone, *tastefied* by a Controler's and Job-Builder's archi-
tecture, for the free-schooling of the sons of the heavy contractors of the
late Demagogue War, to be brought up in idle ignorance.

We have here a word to say on the purposes of our tax-wasting, for they
never are called, as they ought to be, our provident City Fathers. They
are variously, either mechanics, storekeepers, or others, who require
punctuality in their special occupations; and therefore may be supposed
to carry a watch. This they know has a mainspring which directs its
movements; and if no watchmaker were at hand, they would be obliged
to know its construction and working plan, to keep it in serviceable order,
if varied or stopped. They should know it must be so often wound up,
regulated by a balance dial, and the hands to be advanced or retarded
for its accuracy. This watch in denoting time may be taken as an analogy,
on the point of useful knowledge necessary in the cases, to that of the construction and working plan of the human brain, indicating what the human being has to do in its relations to Nature, to others, and to itself. If
watchmakers were gone, the use of our watch would require its mechanism, particularly its movements, with their connections, and agency, to
be known; from the spring that begins the motion, to the hands which
direct us to the occasions for the precise and productive improvement of
our time. The great providential mind-making God and Nature ordained
the human intellect aright. Fictional Schools have ignored or perverted
it. But our rectifying watchmakers of the mind have never yet appeared.
Should not then, this neglected mechanism which holds the mainspring,
and connected influences of human thought and action, be analyzed for
discovering the method of that thought which directs every purpose of
man? Who will gainsay this? It may be answered, the analysis would
be useless; what can be known, is known already, and none know my
mind better than myself. We say, what you have learned of your own

Or at least he'd endeavor, as well as he could,
The examples to furnish, he thought Fogie would;
Or by memory give what he here could not read.
If that is your purpose, said Onward, proceed.

---

mind is very little, and everybody knowing as little, think they know better than you. Do not however mistake your subject. You mean to tell us, only that you may have secret designs unknown to others; while you are totally ignorant of the manner and successions of the process which brought those designs to your perception, and prepared you to act; and whether the action or event will be correspondent to its purpose. But the respondent continues; the mind is such a mysterious agent, that its ways cannot be known, or profound metaphysicians would long ago have discovered them. It is not a spiritual mystery; only an unknown physical fact; and your experience has told you, that working on a fact in the wrong way, will never discover it. The metaphysician instead of penetrating into the light of truth, works only among obscure and blinding clouds. All you know of the mind is something about memory, imagination, reason, judgment and 'logic;' how they are confused and distorted in your thinking and acting, you do not perceive. After so many Geological periods of man passed in the chaos of intellect, it is time to separate and arrange its constituents, to show forth its luminaries, and finally to create a physical Adam-like mind, knowing itself, and comprehending the wisdom and perfection in the works of God and Nature around it.

Now we have something to propose to our worthy Councils. You may not know it, though you are wasting millions by 'political school jobs,' and by schooling calculated to make boys eschew mechanical and useful work, to be idle gentlemen, or with a little flippancy to become sophistical speakers, and ephemeral writers in newspapers and magazines. Take one of your early plain brick school-houses, regardless of externals; for you believe the most sublime truth proceeded from 'a stable and a manger.' Offer a premium for an intelligible physical history of the mind; not regarding what 'people say' who are trading in ignorance of what must supersede their errors. When you get such a history and apply its method without egotistical parade, shouting, dedications, inaugurations, and other College foolery, give sufficient means, for wealth may spoil him, to some observant, reflective, and instructive individual, who has made his mind at home, not his noisy 'mark' in the world. One thousand dollars a year, when paper money is burnt, will thus leave you millions enough, from your Public Schools, to bridge the Schuylkill as often as will be required by 'lot speculators;' and for tickling the vanity of

Master Onward, you magnify matters, but hear,
Their beginning's so puffed-up their end don't appear;
For though Plenty's large lap's filled with fruits and with corn,
She has always a small empty end of her horn.   ·   1130
Then don't promise too largely, or when its time's passed,
Expectation may dwindle to nothing at last.
See your Eminent Borers, self-puffed till they're blind,
And their 'brains growing soft,' from weak use of the mind,
With their vanity striving to bother the Town,
By some Folly set up, or some Wisdom torn down,
To get Newspaper Life, and at Death the proud numeral,
Ten thousand idlers to gape at their funeral.*
Next, count your Rogues, with Three Juries to try them,
Delay, or Twelve men, or a Gold-Wink to buy them.   1140
But vices with us are so fatal, that sure
Your Quack Doctors of Laws can't prevent them or cure :
For although my plain words may seem doubtful to you,
A post-mortem dissection will show it all true.

Shoddy Liveries to eclipse the Vienna Prater, and the Bois de Boulogne,
by the endless dimensions and extravagance of your Fairmount Park.

* Eminent Borers; otherwise miscalled 'Public Spirited Citizens;'
characters scarcely harmless when kept within their own social limit,
but sometimes annoying, if no more, when using the mind on subjects
beyond its capacity; which capacity they cannot measure. They are
generally ambitious to 'start' Societies, as *armies of influence*, and to
'get-up' anything new, that they may be complimented by their dupes,
with being set at the 'head' of it, and to tear down an old commodious
building, to make a parade in laying a New Corner Stone, with their
own name in it. When they join with women to manage National Pau-
perism, their tangling fingers interfere with the broad hand of the rectifying Statesman ; contented with their hope to acquire the name of Good
and Charitable men ; a phrase that should not be received without analysis. The eminent borer's charity, however, wants the Christian ele-
ment ; having no closet work, but all on the house-top. There is no
limit to his City purposes, except through his not being a speech-maker,
which would carry him into Politics with the chance of becoming selfish
and bad.

I've some questions to ask, pardon, if they offend.
Have you found 'Moral Suasion' to answer your end?
Have you lessened your frauds and extravagance yet,
With your Prison doors open to swindling and debt?
Have your Schools and your Churches, beyond what we need,
More than Teacher's and Parson's place-jobbing to plead? 1150
Do you think that the State now more quiet enjoys,
By not punishing rogues, and not whipping bad boys?
Answer these by the fact, throw mere 'Suasion' aside,
Take pure physical thinking, you never have tried;
Like the fanning of wheat, it will winnow the brain
From the chaff of opinions, and heap up the grain.
You've a sad metaphysical swimming of mind,
That will keep you to truth and to steadiness blind,
· With a Tongue-running issue, the plague of the day,
And waste words to say something, with nothing to say; 1160
Taking all your Speech Breath, for the last eighty years,
It would make for the Moon at least two atmosphéres.
Yet to press something from them, the whole you'll condense,
You would get wrangling froth, scarce one clear drop of sense.
By the spell of a planet's delusion you're bound
That may think it runs straight when it only turns 'round.
You are like to those porpoises, Admiral Noah said,
Played 'round his Ark, and yet never would go ahead;
Once 'missing stays' in their tack-about motion,
The slow Fogie Ark got ahead on the ocean. 1170
You think you go forward, take care it's not back;
For you turn on the switch, not advance on the track.
By your doing things cheaply, and all things in haste,
You will do your work badly, and work but to waste;
E'en the Style of your work is 'hotch-potch,' for with you
There is only one rule, to 'get-up' something new;

But to make that new-something, it's needless to say
It must differ from all that is known at the day.
Hence your Taste's a succession of things unrelated,
'Hotch-potch' without principles, as it was stated;   1180
And shows a sad mingling no less to unite
Unharmonious forms, than to join wrong and right,
For Good Taste and Fair-dealing by like rule are made,
Thus distortion mars outline, extortion robs trade.*
Let me here quote a couplet of nursery rhymes,
Which so sadly sets-forth its conditional times.
'If the world were all paper, the water all ink,
'What, alas, should we do for our dinner and drink?'
Why, the Corn Exchange knows by its vested-right union,
That words can raise food, by electric communion;   1190
With chloroformed conscience, on them it behooves
As the grain crop increases to lessen the loaves;
Still if poor-men will give thrice its value in notes,
They'll get one pint of meal for their famishing throats.
And for AUNT NELLY's drink, tariff swindlers have taught her,
There's whisky enough in the place of ink-water.
So now her dear Rib she can counsel anew,
That three hundred per cent upon whisky won't do,
For the Boys have a way, his weak laws can't prevent,
To take what they want down, and throw off the per cent.† 1200

---

* The few succeeding reflections in the Text are given as conclusions
from the related tie of truth, taken from hear-say on forestalling speculation, and nefarious fact, substantiated in opinion by general belief, and
universal indignation.

† Whisky is a colorless fluid; but may resemble some transparent
chemical reagents for superinducing alterations in the character and
color of solutions and bodies; and which by their mutative action may
leave foul stains by its changes. This befouling agent has come to act
upon the United States authority, and has left the deepest die of guilt

Though some go-ahead Yankees may think themselves wise,
We've no microscope-power to see where it lies.
You can't magnify nothing, the thought's almost risible,
Where wisdom is not, glass cannot make it visible.

---

upon it; to the outcry, but scarcely to the surprise, of an upright minority who wish to look upon the Federal Government as having honor and energy to direct its power. It is a notorious case in the Country; still we refer to it here. Four years ago, Congress, in the prosecution of a foolish and disastrous demagogue war, imposed a tax of two dollars a gallon on that besotting drink; the use of which has long degraded the mass of individuals, and which is now become an opprobrium on their Legislative, Judicial, and executive representatives, or their agents. By the statistics of eighteen hundred and sixty, some seventy millions of whisky were distilled in the United States. The tariff on this should have produced some hundred and forty millions of dollars. The Treasury received thirty millions, leaving a deficiency of more than one hundred millions in the last year, and over three hundred millions since the tax was laid. The deserved comment on this, for the culprits cannot be properly punished, if at all, should be, that the great mass of the people are corrupt, or are tainted with indifference, and the Government imbecile, or infected with the like epidemic. But the universal suffrage of an extended population, even if not politically corrupt, will from the confusion of its opinions and interests, become contentious, undetermined, and weak, in its orderly pretensions; and may become wild and ferocious in its anarchical confusion and blindness.

I heard at the time, of a doleful young poet, somewhere along the Mississippi, having worn a deep suit of mourning, on the death of Lord Byron. If he still lives, and is yet as nervous to affliction, he should put on the blushing cloak of shame for the disgrace on the honor and Law of his Country; not to be laid aside till the Official or the offender is brought to punishment.

Frauds on National revenue have been common from the Roman Proconsuls, downwards. Our fellowship of whisky dealers and distillers exceeds those of the other Hemisphere; for ours besides cheating their Government largely, then laugh broadly in its face.

We invite foreign Instructors to our Colleges, and from a dearth of the higher intellect in the Country, perhaps properly. Our Authorities, to amuse themselves with 'something new,' import a few English sparrows, to lessen the swarms of American caterpillars, instead of law-whipping boys from shooting and stoning little birds at home. Ought we not to import some pure, honest, and energetic officers of the Revenue, and

Have wisdom within and a free tongue to show it,
'Twill make its way out to all those who should know it.
If wise as you're called, you'll be able to find
Its true length, breadth, and depth, by strict use of the mind.
You seem wise to Bank-borrow as much as you want,
And then wise not to pay it, by saying you can't ;   1210
You were wise by ' log-rolling,' to buy Forest Logs,
And to poll freemen's votes from Alaska's Ground Hogs.
Now you're wise to get Cuba, by jobbing Promoters
To give Idlers places, by free ' nigger' voters.
Why can't you be shrewd, and pay Knaves the per cent
Without jobbing, and thus save the Capital spent?*

---

change them for a new set, before they have time, from bad example, to
turn demagogues, or become loafers on the Treasury?

* The United States, if they can be united, would, to practical calculation, seem to have unimproved and unimprovable land enough to occupy
its locomotive idlers, gold hunters, and other speculators, for the next
hundred years. Not so indeed. Demagogues and broken-down Politi-
cians having served the People to the wearing out of their tongue, turn
their wits to serve themselves, by living on a percentage for 'services
rendered,' in forwarding UNCLE SAM's heavy contracts for Territory, or
its ignorant or savage sovereign People; to which extravagance however, our frugal AUNT NELLY, with her lap full of debt, presents a useless veto. A great Job has lately ' come off' so profitably, with the pine
forests, snows, and earth-housed Indians of Alaska, that the Jobbers are
' up for' a high percentage with Cuba. During the Southern filibuster-
ing intrigue for the *Queen of the Antilles,* to increase our slave population,
one of the Northern speech-makers, with a view to eventual abolition,
figuratively said, give ' manifest destiny' her time, and sugar plantations,
' niggers' and all will ' gravitate' into the Union. Now the advocates of
negro freedom and negro suffrage are desirous the gravitation should
come-on at once; but the percentage Jobbers perceive the velocity would
be hastened by laying a hundred millions of heavy gold, plus the knave's
pay, on the back of the Island. If this should fail, might not Congress
again ' get-up' the Soap-Bubble mission, for the purchase of Saturn's
Ring? It would afford percentage to the Jobbers, and to stock and bank-
ing Operators a ' first-rate' investment in a smooth and brilliant rail-
road, for American ' Excursionists' to make a summer, or sleighing cir-

You seem wise to be lazy on Office and friend,
For without these your days would in poverty end;
You seemed once Balloon-wise, 'mid the Camp's silly shout,
Till your enemies' jokes cracked your bag of wind out.   1220
And you lastly are wise unto foolishness, when
You find out you're not wise and would hide it from men.
Recollect mighty Cæsar, 'mid glory's mad glare,
Never turned to or heeded his death-word, ' beware.'
So when God's sign to Noah for Gopherwood passed,
They derided his Ark, and caroused to the last,
For their trumpery adding to credit's long score,
At some Antediluvian Chesnut street store;
'Till the crisis came on, and the panic ensued,
And both debtor and creditor sunk in the flood;   1230
While the Deluge washed off, with their marriage and mirth,
All the sins of mankind from the face of the earth.
Like the Rogue's Bankrupt act, by Congressional power,
Decreed a Soap-Flood their pollutions to scour,
Then washing their stains out with Law-bleaching skill,
That you hardly would know they had passed thro' the mill;
Since to blot all distinctions from jealousy's eyes,
We must call the knave honest, the foolish call wise.
As through Liberty's cloud we are all alike seen,
Black and white, clean and dirty, the noble and mean;   1240
And in this favored land of Equality, each
Is the other, as strict nouns of multitude teach;
We're alike in our notions of Freedom and Rights,
In like thinking, vain boasting, and hunger for Sights,

---

cuit, to 'go ahead' and to see 'something new,' on that unexplored
Planet. It 'would pay' 'first come only served' speculators, as well as
the South Sea Bubble.

In our vagabond gadding, and mania to roam
Here and there after something, to keep us from home.
We may get rid of time by this quick change of place,
But we can't change ourselves, Nature settles that case.
Oh how horrible then, varied Climes scrambled o'er,
To come back with our own vapid self as before.*   1250

---

* As the meaning of the summary reflections that follow in the Text, on Demagogue rule and practice, may be more clearly stated in prose, we here offer some prefatory remarks, derived from observation of the working plan of the American Representative Government.

We begin with the undeniable assertion, founded on experience, that man cannot govern himself; nor be governed well, except, if that is possible, by the diffusion of the highest kind of knowledge, that of the mind which governs; and by its wise and upright application. Two plans, under equal ignorance and ambition, have been severally tried without success, in Republics, and Monarchies. The proposal of a general Democracy, being merely a metaphysical notion: observation and reflection have accorded in the maxim, that the universal people must exercise its ruling power by Representation. It would not be difficult to show, by brief analysis, the gradual manner in which the good-natured people, when few in number, first yield their opinion to others ; and afterwards, without themselves knowing it, are brought to a state of slavish submission under a few or a majority. A part of the mutual relation between the Demagogue and the People, when thus controled, I would here briefly describe.

When Parties of the People are sheep-like driven by their respective Demagogues, the representative elections are carried on in the usual manner of thoughtless and vulgar contentions, by abuse, slander, falsehood, and every sort of opprobrium, from one party and its leaders, on the other. In this case, the leaders on each side rule their adherents by despotic craft; and the respective parties implicitly submit to their selfish knavery : leaders and parties on the two sides, ferociously hating each other. But the respective leaders ruling the whole Country between themselves, are contented to hold this divided empire; for the Country cannot be ruled by a single Oligarchy. Sometimes however, one party or both become dissatisfied with their leaders. Then the leaders, alarmed for their divided authority, and seemingly reconciled, join their powers, that each may preserve or regain his own. When this threatened danger passes by, the inter-enmity revives, and each returns to his separate party rule. This attempt at disorganization is always occurring in individual

We would choose too, to be all alike in our votes,
But a party-edged knife, only fit to cut throats,
Takes our single intention and cuts it in two;
Yet by Truth's analytic unprejudiced view,

---

cases, when a disappointed office-seeker leaves his own party for the other side. Such instances do not alarm the double oligarchy and its respective party, for the reciprocal loss balances itself. Occasionally however a seditious dissatisfaction taking place in one or both the parties may cause a general opposition to the leaders. Then a unanimous or majorative oligarchy is formed of the leaders on both sides, to resist, by their united authority, the threatening independence of the people. This general revolt has occurred twice in the course of the Republic.

The first happened previously to the election of the Seventh President. The thought of taking an uneducated, in its best meaning, and ignorant soldier for a Chief Magistrate, threw the opinion of the people off its habitual pivot; and the parties showing a disposition to shake off their harness, the leaders or rather drivers, whether Federal, Democratic, Whig, Federal Republican, or under the names of various leaders, all united into one new and overwhelming party, to put the government into the incompetent hands of a Military Officer. This gave the combined Oligarchical rule to the leaders of all parties · which continued for eight years of its reign; and then resolved into new opponent parties.

The last revolt against the leaders occurred at the beginning of the Southern Rebellion. At this time parties were divided under the several names of Democrats, Republicans, Slavery and Anti-Slavery, Freesoilers, Abolition Fanatics, State Rights, and Broken Platforms. The contests on these points disgusting the people, they all, except the Southern insurrectionists, formed one overpowering Oligarchy under the name of Union Republicans. The imbecility and corruption of this Oligarchy have brought back one set of these old party leaders, who uniting themselves with the insurrectionists are using every form of Lawyer-sophistry to enable a conquered people to rule those who conquered them: making it appear that a bloody war, long provoked, and an enormous debt incurred in the twinkling of an eye, was 'got-up' by Southern Demagogues, and Abolition Fanatics of the North, to make the whole country look like a maimed and floundering fool, doomed perhaps to some greater calamity.

This Note is addressed to the sufferers under the political condition of the Country. The Demagogue will not herein recognize himself. Passing with his party, for the greatest man of the moment; and being too vain to observe or reflect, except upon his ambition, he acts without comprehending the instinct that attends and directs the urgent passion of con-

You'll perceive 'tis the Demagogue's miscreant art,
To yoke Freedom's winged steeds to his voting dog-cart.
And though fiercely they now growling-talk at each other,
One point they agree-on as brother with brother;
For should anything happen to question their choice,
In directing the people's proud Democrat voice,   1260
Then each side, taking fright for its safety and ends,
Would unite for a time to be treacherous friends;
And like partnership wolves, for their now threatened cause
Draw in both flocks of sheep, for their friendly-grown jaws;
Till in time the flocks pacified, each to its fold,
Leave the wolves to make ready their teeth as of old.
Then dissolving their partnership, still so contrive
To make flock war with flock, on their quarrels to thrive;
And as wrangling will lead the sheep people astray,
There'll be vote-famished vultures to make us their prey.   1270
Yet the sheep though secure, give the shearers no quiet,
To fleece his own flock each again turns to try-it.
Since Demogogue-itching, of what ever side,
Is to take all the wool, up to shaving the hide.

To return from this Party division by name,
Where the Law and our wishes would make us the same,

---

ceit. His little intellect is so limited to himself that we would liken it to
that of the sub-animal. But its instinct is proper because it is Natural;
his is so perverted or false, that besides doing mischief, it prevents him
from perceiving in that mischief a picture of himself.

It is the disgust of portions of the People who might be able to influence an election, which has produced a disposition to turn from the
notorious profligacy of trading political Demagogues, to any candidate
for the higher gifts of suffrage who may negatively at least, appear to be
free from their bare-faced vices, and selfish incompetency. In the choice
of a Chief Magistrate, we willingly take with hope, an improvable, or
corrigible ignorance, serious as it might be in a civil or military character, to an utterly unchangeable and incurable dishonesty.

To the life then, Equality's mask is so true,
That between knave and saint, you can't say who is who.
Hence in these kind, forgiving, and pharisee times,
We want branding, to tell man from man by his crimes;   1280
When the clerk and cashier, by protection made bold,
And the briber and bribed, swear the secret to hold;
When the loafer in hopes of compassion, offends
Against kindly relations, and word-trusting friends;
Or when final contrition spread over with cant,
Makes a fall from the gallows a rise of the Saint.*
Thus the blood of a household, atrociously shed,
And eight lives at one swoop by one foul villain sped,
With the twice-seeming death, of a brain-dashing fate,
And of throat-cutting gashes, alike to the eight;   1290
On his own free confession, to think you could find
A defender of such an unhorrified mind
As to use the Bar-Sophistry vainly to draw
Such a cobweb of argument 'round the stern Law;
Hear it too! how his Priest, as Earth's counsel had failed,
Gave the Counsel of Heaven, when death had prevailed
On the monster to say, since life's sinning was o'er,
Under true gallows' seal, that he'd now sin no more;
And though mercy sent up his black heart white as snow,
God has hid his red hand in its grave here below.   1300

---

* Three years previously to the date of this Note, the justice and compassion of the community were equally shocked by the atrocity which the succeeding lines of the Text record. An emigrant Dutchman, with a deluded hope of gain, murdered at a farm-house near Philadelphia, the heads of a family, four children, including an infant, and two inmates, by the double assurance of the axe and of the knife. But this wretch, though confessing part of his crime, taken to be innocent, before being proved by circumstances to be guilty, *must have* two appointed counsel, to sophisticate his case; and more than one Priest to mummerize his salvation. He was only hanged!

If a Fogie is not always prudent, at least
You'd found none in this case to be Lawyer or Priest;
When whole chapters of crimes through life's sinful edition,
Can't weigh against three thoughtless words of contrition.*

  Awake, dreaming Go-ahead, look at your Country,
In debt deep to drowning, yet still with effront'ry
Of pride and of vanity, needing the rod,
And the hypocrite's canting, the vengeance of God.
You will find these in Churches, and national Halls,
But to tell the truth there, you'll address empty walls;   1310
So it's safe to avoid all ill-tempered commotions,
By wrangling on old metaphysical notions.
Again should just Heaven not blot us out quite,
For official corruption, and all that's not right;
Yet to see money-dealers as once scourged of old,
Although now for vile paper, as then for fine gold,
We may think of God's wrath in the temple and flood,
And perhaps frequent whipping may do us some good.
Thus it has been ordained, for renewing old fears,
To raise Panic's wide windows some every ten years,   1320
And for God's wiser purpose, not drown us to death,
In the sea of our crimes, and at once stop our breath;
But to let us swim through, and, unwarned by the pain,
Try, like rats escaped drowning, our mischief again;
So to save death by choking, all seeming hope passed,
Like a suicide pig cut our own throat at last.

---

  * The preceding lines of the Text are satiric sketches founded on the
related tie of truth; or where derived from fainter degrees of relation,
they are given as only a slightly overdrawn picture. The succeeding
and terminating rhymes, together with the strictly connected images of
truth, contain those fainter degrees of the tie, which produce a perception
of the odd, the ludicrous, and the extravagant.

He was going to read further, when Onward turned 'round,
With his knees doubled up, and prepared for a bound,
A strange figure to meet that appeared as it flew,
Like a double-winged hurricane, ' something quite new,'   1330
With its cloud-cleaving cap ; to its foot a wheeled skate,
And if fleetness can time and space ánnihilate,
By one quick jump between them, 'twould seem but a span,
Leaping straight out of Bersheba right into Dan.
He's the winged Priest of Progress, said ONWARD, whose will
Would make all but his purposes seem to stand still.
I've an errand on hand, it lies right in his way
To the President-Platform, in meeting to-day ;
Where they've all got to sixes and sevens, it's said,
And the world will be lost if they can't go ahead.   1340
So good-by, Mr. Rhymster, I'll hitch to his flight,
Then on seizing his skirts was at once out of sight.
What they're after they know not ; we seek not in vain,
Yet as every one's made in the mould of his brain,
Learn its physical structure and true working plan,
Or you'll never know God's wise intention in man.
Train the mind up awake, it will be what it seems,
Free from mad metaphysic sophistical dreams ;
For what does not exist, and which cannot be taught,
Is in each an impossible purpose of thought.   1350
But these Go-aheads still have false Folly in view,
Which with foot and tongue running they'd call wise and true.
Let the Genius of Progress then ply his swift wings,
After what are called new, sometimes ruinous things ;
As he sees not his failures in all that has passed,
He must break his own neck and the Country's at last.

    Thus a Land under Party will always be led
By a selfish ambition whose tongue runs ahead ;

Still it's ignorance all, with the led and the leader,
For both live on words, one the fed, t'other feeder;   1360
And should you not manage their bond to dissever,
Take knave and fool's government on you forever.
While go-too-fast Nations, self-spurred in the race,
Though they've action enough, yet it's all out of place.
Give them wisdom's staid curb, and her sure guiding rein,
Or their whip and their spur will be wrong or in vain;
But without her direction, they'll ride to the fate
Of the Beggar on Horseback, go soon or go late.

THE END.